# Ship of Fools

*"The world wants
to be deceived."*

Sebastian Brant,
*The Ship of Fools,* 1494

# Ship of Fools

## Stories from the Mental Health Front Line

*Rod Madocks*

Five Leaves Publications

www.fiveleaves.co.uk

**Ship of Fools**
by Rod Madocks

Published in 2013
by Five Leaves Publications,
PO Box 8786, Nottingham NG1 9AW
www.fiveleaves.co.uk

Five Leaves acknowledges
financial support from
Arts Council England

Cover copyright © Leon de Bliquy,
www.leondebliquy.com

Title page illustration taken from
*Narrenschiff* by Sebastian Brant
published in 1494

Typesetting and design by
Four Sheets Design and Print

Printed by Imprint Digital in Exeter

# Contents

Introduction — Ship of Fools 7

The Break 10

The Wrong Arm 16

*Primum Non Nocere* 19

The Cure 37

The Rescue 43

The Practice of Deliverance 52

Good Morning, Death 62

The Terror 73

Transference 79

The Killing 89

The Stillness, the Dancing 99

The New Recruit 106

One in Seven 114

From a Distance 123

Brilliant 126

The Fire Game of Nil 130

Nor Shall It Sleep in My Hand 140

The Price 151

The Happiest Country Has No History 159

The Drowned and the Saved 165

# Introduction –
# Ship of Fools

I've seen them on the water under the moon's stigmata. Drifting downstream, all sorts of folk: some embracing their lovers, others playing a tune, or bent to a studded crucifix, else screaming as the minnows tore at them. All clinging to the same craft with their faces lit by the bony lunar shine. The river swept them on. In my heart I wanted to join them.

The Ship of Fools had been with me a long time. Years ago I came across it on the wall of the staff meeting room of a maximum security mental health hospital. A print of a Dürer woodcut. The dirty business of the hospital churned in that room. We ran a complex secretive machine to contain six hundred dangerous cases. The gradient of the day would be sharpened by the crick-crack of magnetic locks and the rasp of key chains as staff came and went. Discussions and arguments raged about patient transfers, security updates and the best new therapeutic approaches to take. There'd be the usual clattering of antlers between the medics and the ebb and flow of departmental politics. Often, cauterised by all the talk, I'd set my gaze on that picture. I liked looking into its elliptical depths and making out all the crazy little figures. I was always seeing something new. I wondered what knowing mind had arranged for it to be hung there in the first place. Maybe it had been placed to remind us that despite the seeming order and purpose of our work we were often as mad as the patients and full of the self-love and delusional thinking that made us all fit for the Ship of Fools.

Five centuries ago the Hanseatic cities along the Rhine found an expedient by which they would pack up all their lunatics and the feeble-minded into boats. These *narrenschiffe* would drift down to the next city, with moon-blanched sails under a bald sky. I came to realise that there were many versions of the Ship of Fools. There was a new one for each generation, but the vessels took the same mazy course. These particular stories are another rendition. I've tried to hold the camera steady and bring back a true account.

There was also a perverse freedom in the Ship of Fools. You could do anything you liked on that vessel. I often wished that liberty for my own patients, trapped as they were by new exquisite punishments. Not straight-jackets and Bedlam but: new drugs, cognitive therapy, neuroscience, slick corporate healthcare, patient-centred practice and all. I wished sometimes that they could keep on sailing — good mad fools — to escape those who would claim them body and soul.

What is a career? Memories, dreams and uncertainties which the passage of time has deformed into certainties. I came to psychiatry wanting to be taught how to live. Instead I found that mental illness was a squalid, degrading business. All that I learned came from the intense humanity of the patients. These stories reflect my career as a mental health worker in institutions and out on the streets. There is a story here for each year that I so laboured. I did not begrudge the work. It was an education *nonpareil*. You should not trust the artist, but I tell you that these stories draw on real events. All this happened.

*Rod Madocks*

# The
# Break

Transient *psychotic episode — unknown aetiology.* That's what it said about her in the notes. She was a young woman sitting upright and alone in the acid yellow light of the triage rooms. Her eyes slowly traversed the wall that faced her as if trying to pick up some meaning in the slight imperfections in the paintwork. The emergency rooms were full of racket and movement as anxious relatives besieged the scurrying staff for news but she remained untouched by the turmoil, just staring at the wall.

The woman's husband paced outside. He was not happy about her being seen by mental health staff.

"She is not mad — just a normal mum," I heard him saying.

The emergency room med staff briefed us. She had come in by ambulance at 19.00 hours. Disorientated in place and time. Colles' fracture of the right wrist. It was bent like an old dinner fork. They had x-rayed and manipulated the arm and put it in a backslab plaster. She had showed no awareness of pain at all even though the limb was red and swollen. The husband had been particularly frightened by her lack of pain.

Now the soma was sorted out it was time for psychiatry to lend a hand.

"She's probably had some sort of psychotic break," said the emergency department house officer.

"Two breaks, poor thing," observed the ward staff-nurse pointing to her wrist.

We took her to psychi admission — several floors up in that big general hospital. She remained silent, acquiescent and incurious. We moved her in a wheelchair as if she had somehow forgotten how to walk. Once in an interview room, we took a closer look at her. She had a raw gaze, unpeeled in some way. Her eyes just passed through you. She was young with a pleasant, unremarkable face. Thick hair cut into a chestnut bob. Fragments of wood, grass and leaves kept dropping onto the interview room table whenever she moved her head. Occasionally, she lifted her hand up to touch her face as if checking that it was still there. Her fingers were scratched, scorched and bloodied. Her knuckles looked as if she had been in a fist fight. There was a bruise under the right eye. Shreds of dried froth clung to her lips. She usually wore specs but no one knew what had happened to them. She kept her stained blouse on with a hospital gown thrown over it. Bare feet stuck out of ripped jeans. Not fashionably torn. There were bloodied rents and gashes all over her legs.

We tried speaking to her. She attempted to focus but struggled to find any words. All she could do was to give us a shrug and a frightened smile. She was like a person who had been swept up into the eye of a hurricane, whirled around at its ferocious centre then slammed down again.

The other ward inhabitants scuffled past the interview room doors. These were our standard fare — the evidently ill — those whom we had successfully categorized, the functional and the affective illnesses, the schizophrenics and the depressives. They gathered in a straggling line by the medication trolley. One man remained lying on the lavatory floor with the door open; he had headphones on and was singing in a cracked voice.

Her husband looked horrified at suddenly finding himself in this place. It took a while to settle him down and get him to tell us what had happened that evening.

They lived in the suburbs and had been married for six years. They had two small boys who were doing well. Happy? Yes of course, they were happy and settled. He worked in insurance and she kept the home and looked after the kids. They had recently bought a newly-built executive home with a conservatory. Nice views of the city. No problems or illnesses, no financial or other concerns — a normal young family. His wife had shown no outward sign of distress. It was a weekday evening. She liked to work in the kitchen while watching a small TV. Cookery and dance competition programmes mainly. A casserole was warming in the oven. No one had really noticed anything unusual. At some stage she had gone into the conservatory. A soft dusk was settling and the streetlights had just come on.

The first they had heard was the crash of the conservatory glass going. She went right through as if she had taken a run at it and gone full tilt. The husband was just in time to see her bounding across the lawn. She disappeared into the freshly-planted flower border and began to smash at the fencing with a fierce strength. She somehow managed to prize off several planks with her bare hands and pushed through the gap. He had chased out after her and called, "Anne!" But she had already gone and crashed down a steep sandstone bank beyond their garden, a wilderness area thickly overgrown with holly and nettle. She emerged under streetlights thirty feet down. Then dashed onto a busy suburban road, hurdled the traffic barriers and ran straight through two lanes of traffic without stopping. Cars tyres yelped as drivers swung to avoid her. The husband could hear their frightened shouts. She leaped over another metal traffic barrier, went smash through a privet hedge then right across another garden, a dog chasing her through a mesh of washing lines. Still she ran on bare-footed. Those naked feet kicked at another fence leaving a star-shaped hole in the woven boards. Out onto a last lamp-lit stretch of pavement, sprinting on rough tarmac, caught in bright light for an instant then smack into the front of an oncoming commercial van.

Her husband found her lying stunned in the road, her wrist twisted at an odd angle but with her eyes still open and intent. Luckily the van driver had seen her wild fleeing shape and had applied the brakes. She made no sound as she lay there and seemed to feel no pain. Her husband had followed her trail of destruction through the estate. It was as if a boulder had rolled through suburbia, all the neighbours and their children milling about in her wake.

She said later that at the time she was filled with unreasoning terror and was running from something unknown as if her life depended on it. She had never experienced such a thing before and had no explanation for it. Her husband was reluctant to agree to us sectioning her and she made no active attempt to leave the ward so she remained a voluntary patient. We applied all the blunt formulaic tools of psychiatry to try and put a label to her problem. We delved into her family history but could find no hint of schizophrenia or any mental illness. She did not have any abnormal beliefs or perceptions. If she had been fleeing due to a delusional process then there was no longer any evidence of it. Her mood seemed normal. There were no drug or alcohol problems. Blood hormone tests and liver function tests came back within an average range. She had shown no mental problems during her pregnancies — usually a litmus test for psychiatric vulnerability. She sat in the ward review while we all questioned her to no avail. Beyond the dusty ward windows a jolting autumn wind blew the first falling leaves into the hospital ornamental pond. We could just hear the wind-ragged spatter of the fountain through the insulated glass.

She stayed on the ward for a few more days. She was frightened of the other patients and kept asking when she could leave. They brought her children to see her, two plump little boys who stood outside by the pond area, holding their father's hands and waving to her from outside. They didn't want them to get contaminated by actually going onto the ward. All the while she remained with us her skin abrasions began to repair themselves, the break in her arm starting to mend and the web of her ordinary perceptions also seemed to knit back together. She spoke steadily and sensibly about her hopes and plans for returning to everyday life. We continued to search for what had caused that extraordinary rent in her reality and began to cast about among the more unusual causes for psychosis. Was it some sort of infarct? No, a scan excluded that. Toxoplasmosis from the family cats? Blood tests showed no parasite infection. Nor was it a dissasociative state caused by toxicity. We also eliminated metabolic, endocrine and infective agents as causes for her episode of derangement. Nothing. When physical causation yielded no results we tried hard to find evidence that this had been a psychodynamic phenomenon, some violent psychological upswell, a seismic revolt against stifling domestic unhappiness. But the answer was the same. She seemed to be happy, well adjusted and all relations were unproblematic.

We needed to find something because we were all frightened by her. Not understanding what had happened to her somehow put us all at risk. We didn't want to be left with the notion of some inexplicable arbitrary terror just waiting inside to explode. There was a reluctance to accept that our patient was an enigmatic time-bomb. It was as if this quiet housewife exemplified all the great human mysteries, the strange disappearances, the Mary Celeste and everything. That human capacity to go completely insane without warning or explanation and with untold consequences. We imagined a future for her husband and family of just waiting, wondering if and when it would happen again.

We let her go after one last case review. We watched her leave, looking down from the ward windows. Her husband shepherded her out, holding a plastic bag with her night clothes and wash things. Her sons clambered into the back of the car. She sat in the front passenger seat, her arm folded carefully into a sling. There was a sudden scurry of autumn leaves, the wavering white thread of the fountain sent scuds of froth onto the hospital drive. They drove away. She seemed to be staring fixedly ahead as the car nosed into the moiling traffic.

# The Wrong Arm

It was a terrible thing to lose a right arm. Especially for a right-handed man. We had all agreed on that but the physio demurred. We paused to let her explain her position. We had known her for years in the high secure facility; she was wise and well respected. The long-term staff often developed an almost mystic sagacity that came from dealing with such problematic patients over the years. She insisted that to lose a right arm in a right-handed man was not necessarily a disaster. It could be seen as an opportunity, a new start in life. She said that a right-handed man punched his way through life. He cleaved his space with that dominant arm but, she argued, now our new amputee patient would have the chance of leading with his left and finding an alternative feminine way. He would now be able to feel or stroke his way in the world instead of hacking and hewing. Yes, he would palpate his path in life like an ant, a careful, peaceable queen-ruled ant. We liked the idea. She had silenced us hard-bitten forensic professionals. We had been discussing the admission of a new patient called Desmond to maximum security. It was intriguing to think that we could possibly take a new therapeutic tack with him. That physio had reproached us for our clichéd thinking and we felt the better for her optimism.

Unfortunately Desmond proved the physio very wrong. We realised soon after he had arrived that he was obstinately aggressive regardless of his disability. He seemed to be formed of rage to the bone. He'd lost his right arm because he had some irrational grudge against the transport system; he had assaulted rail staff then in a psychotic frenzy had leapt into the path of an oncoming train brandishing his fist. The train had duly taken his arm off although this had not dampened his fury. Transferred to us, he remained consumed with wrath; even on his good days he'd prowl his cell all coiled up and ready to strike. If you glanced into his hot mad eyes for a moment he'd yell, "Doan look at me like that, man," and more often than not would lunge at the battered perspex doors of the restraint cell.

The hospital fitted him with a replacement arm. It had a coal-black rubbery hand darker than his actual colour. We soon realised that was a mistake. His tendency was to unstrap his arm and belabour patients and staff with it like a club. If he was particularly riled up, he would unscrew the hand to reveal a knurled brass thread which he would deploy as a pointed spike, using the arm like a spear to gouge at unprotected faces. Often he became so hard to manage that we would have to take his arm away altogether.

I guess for Desmond any arm was going to be the wrong arm, for some men, although change is the order of the world, they themselves are fixed in their essence, fixed to a bitter core.

# Primum Non Nocere

Firstly, do no harm. The words came from the Hippocratic Oath. They were occasionally cited during our training. We could all swear to the principle at the outset. There must have been very few hard-boiled ones who had actually set out to do hurt from the beginning. More often it just seemed that the work graunched down on susceptible personalities and that brought the harm. The mischief already done by their illnesses was bad enough for the patients and this was often combined with the evil that the system inflicted upon them. They had drawn low cards in the lottery of life to get mental illness in the first place and then they had us to deal with on top of that.

What motivated us to take on the work also guided our hands as to how we treated the patients. Many came because the work built them up and gave them power, a few were genuinely altruistic. Some needed to heal their own distress, others came out of curiosity, yet more arrived just by accident. Then there were those who could get no alternative work. The patients would have done anything to avoid us. They instinctively knew that it was best not to be netted up in the psychiatric system at all. Unfortunately, few of our patients' infirmities would have improved with nothing being done for them though some life crises would have resolved in time. A few depressions and anxieties would have bubbled away without too much distress. Psychosis, however, fed off itself and rarely improved without help and manias were an ever-ascending stair. There were those who tried to cure themselves with prayer or holistic therapies, by family love or by self-medicating through drugs and alcohol. The results were rarely successful.

Occasionally sufferers tried to hide away from us until the madness had passed. I knew a Sikh man with severe bipolar illness. He took himself off to India to try a temple cure. He told me that four monks accompanied him everywhere for weeks and made him run up and down hills. They also had him drink daily from a black treacly-looking mixture of curative herbs. His mental health did improve quite a bit. He kept the bottles of the black stuff in his fridge when he got back but the juice ran out in the end. He then began to deteriorate and eventually fell back into our hands again. They all came back through that narrow gate, usually. Over the years, the same names kept returning onto the case lists, late or soon. We did much good for people but often the cure was as bitter as the affliction.

The harm was obvious from the start when I first entered the wards. You would see the corridors lined with shivering, rocking and quaking human beings. These were the ones affected by the side effects of the medication. We even called one characteristic form of locomotion — "The Modecate Shuffle" after the type of injectable medicine that caused it. If you were on the stuff long enough you could get the feared tardive dyskinesia, an incurable affliction which made you shake uncontrollably for good. The long-term patients took on a stiffened, palsied, shuffling gait with saliva constantly drooling. Many kept crossing and re-crossing their legs, or hopping from one leg to the other. Others would twist or rotate their arms back and forth the whole time, their faces involuntarily puckering and pouting. In others, their tongues could flicker and flip about in their mouths like lizards. Some held their hands out in a cup shape and kept rubbing their fingers together in a rhythmic manner called 'pill-rolling' by the clinicians. I remember finding one young woman lying on the floor completely seized up and unable to move at all. Some men grew breasts and fluid ran from the nipples of men and women. New generations of anti-psychotic drugs came along called the 'atypicals'. These were supposed to have fewer side effects than the old poisonous drugs yet these, in time, showed their shadow side with a legacy of excessive weight gain and reduced libido, conferring diabetes and strokes on otherwise healthy young adults, or else giving them wheezy, spongy lungs and debilitating blood diseases.

It was startling how quickly a person became an inmate. That lean, street-savvy young person you admitted could within a short while be transformed into a pumpkin-faced creature, vague-eyed, shorn of memory, speaking with a drawling voice and scuffling in his slippers at the ward office door, pestering the staff for one more ciggie from his hourly ration.

I started work in a large Victorian mental hospital and one of my jobs was to take papers to the medical records office. This office was buried deep in the institution and was reached by passing through a long corridor lined with steam pipes from the heating system. Here in winter the long-term patients, evicted from the wards during the day, congregated in the warm fug. Dozens of them lay on the floor smoking or drowsing, their backs to the hot pipes. The staff hurrying along down the corridor had to step over their legs.

At some stage in its ninety-year history tropical crickets had colonised the heating vents of the place. A muted chirping could be heard all day and night. The sound of the crickets merged with the murmured greetings of the patients in the corridor as you passed by them. This created a lulling effect. Sometimes I felt like lying down alongside them and also embracing oblivion. The hospital was eventually closed, as so many were. The heating system was shut down. The crickets died within a short time and all grew silent, not unlike many of the patients sent out to wither away and perish in lonely boarding houses and bedsits. Such was community care.

The survivors often longed to return to those wards and whole populations of ex-patients often still lived like ghost communities around the sites of the old defunct asylums. I once had to deal with an ex-long-termer who kept presenting with unusual infections that landed him back in hospital. He seemed very happy to be back on the wards and kept being readmitted until I caught him one day packing his own shit into an empty Biro tube and blowing the stuff into a hole in his leg that he had made himself.

As for my own personal role in all this mayhem, most of the harm I did in the early days came from sheer incompetence. I remember going to an acute renal unit to assess a man who had become disturbed and confused, and while manoeuvring next to the transfusion unit I tripped and accidentally pulled out a trailing plastic pipe. Jets of thick yellow liquid started pumping out the end of the tube. The patient went very quiet as I tried unsuccessfully to stick the thing back in. Alarm bells began to ring and all of sudden the poor man had far worse symptoms to worry about. That particular patient survived my clumsy feet, but in general we went about our duties with careless insouciance and little training. I recall helping colleagues to restrain agitated patients any-old-how, just grabbing on to legs and arms until the trousers would be dragged down and an injection given. We would then troop off to the office for a ciggie and a cup of tea. Sometimes we'd give our smokes to the patients to commiserate.

The worst places for blatant abuse were the residential units for learning disability. On an early shift at one of those places when we were dividing up the work to be done before breakfast, one male assistant said to me with a wink, "You dress the males and I'll dress the females, especially the pretty ones." I did not trouble myself overmuch at the time and just rattled along full of youthful confidence that I could cope with anything.

That is probably why I volunteered to take a group of patients to a holiday camp near Yarmouth one summer. I drove the specially adapted vehicle and family and staff waved us off. One pair of timid, worried parents told me that this was the first time their son Billy had been away from them and they asked me to take special care of him. Billy was a heavily-built, shambling six footer with a curly beehive of hair. He waddled along in outsize trousers that covered the giant nappies he wore all the time. He had no speech and just made gurgling noises. I reassured the parents that Billy would be fine and he followed me to his seat tamely enough. Things began to go awry during the first stop somewhere in Lincolnshire.

I took Billy to the lavatories and inserted him in a stall. I reluctantly peered inside when he started to make frenzied noises and found that he was unable to take his own trousers down. I squeezed inside and was dismayed to see that he was so tightly encased in his nappy that the only way I could find to get it off was to kneel down in front of him and yank at it from below. After a good deal of struggling accompanied by much bellowing and groaning from Billy I managed to free him from his bindings and emerged, somewhat dishevelled, from the stall to find a group of truckers staring in horror, "It shouldn't be allowed. That shouldn't," I heard one ranting in my wake.

The situation was not improved when another of our party lobbed a full coke bottle through a window of the café. I slapped down some money to cover the damage, retrieved Billy from the latrines and bundled everyone back on the bus. We roared off without further ado.

I was relieved to arrive at the camp with no further mishap and settled my charges into their shared accommodation. All seemed set fair. On the first morning Billy spied the camp open-air swimming pool and made it known by grunts and gestures that he wanted a swim. I didn't worry too much about the fact that he had no swimming costume. The other clients were all sunning themselves safely on deck chairs. I borrowed a voluminous pair of trunks off one of them and smilingly ushered Billy to the pool. All was quiet apart from the bubbling of the pump. No-one else was about. The pool looked quite small. I sat on a low wall, opened a beer can and fired up a B & H. Billy advanced to the water wagging his head from side to side like a penguin. He firmly grasped the chrome stair rails and methodically descended. He looked happy and seemed to enjoy the cool blue waters slowly rising to his waist. Down he went while I nodded encouragement. All of a sudden he went completely out of sight.

There was a churning and bubbling on the surface of the water. He came back up just once, his face all red and bulging and with his eyes staring back at me in mute terror. His mouth opened and he took in a great draught of water. I was already pulling off my shoes and bounding to the side of the pool but he had sunk to the bottom by then. The pool was much deeper than I had thought. I jumped straight in and swam down to him. He was in a sitting position on the bottom, his hair streaming like weed. As soon as I tried to tug him upwards his great hands shot out and grabbed me. I struggled but the combination of my heavy clothes and his powerful hold began to overwhelm me. I remember having a very distinct notion that I was going to drown in that pool alongside him unless I did something drastic. I drew back my fist and punched him twice in the belly as hard as I could. He let go and emitted a storm of bubbles. I came up, got a breath, then tried to swim up with him but he was so huge and sodden I hadn't the strength to shift him.

Somehow I got the idea of actually standing on the bottom of the pool with him on my shoulders. This seemed to work and I slowly crabbed my way towards the shallow end taking him with me. At last we broke into air and I lugged him towards the shallow end ladder. He seemed to be completely unresponsive. The word "inquest" was echoing in my head as I got under him and hiked him up onto the concrete lip of the pool. A minute of frantic CPR and he began to gush water like a broken hydrant. He sat up and began coughing and rocking back and forth.

"How are you doing, Billy?" I asked fearfully. His vacant eyes looked queasy and he rubbed at his guts where I had punched him. The sunlight played tranquilly on us and little pied wagtails skittered about on the paving next to the pool as if nothing had happened. He made a muted groaning noise.

"That was some swim, eh, Billy?" I said after a while. "Let's give it a rest for now. I don't think you're cut out for it. It will be our little secret. Shush now." I put my finger to my lips. Billy made a noise like a sea-lion. I think it was him laughing. He used to honk like that throughout the rest of the holiday whenever I made that shushing gesture to him. He seemed to experience no lasting ill effects and I returned him to his parents with a breezy report on how well he had done. My terror subsided gradually. I knew that I'd gone near the edge though.

My career developed. I was given more responsibility and began to shed any remaining idealism about the job, yet I retained the idea that I could manage anything that was thrown at me. I became a shift leader in a residential unit for troubled teens and young disabled people. I worked rotating day and night shifts. At night I was pretty much on my own. That was when the mayhem went on. Some residents fought with each other, the more able preyed on the weaker ones. I got used to cutting corners and taking risks. I remember one young man who had kept me up for hours holding a blade to his own throat and threatening to cut. In the end I told him to just get on with it as I needed to take a nap. He looked so startled that he put the knife down for a moment and I took the opportunity of snatching the blade from him. I sent him to bed and did not trouble to inform anyone of the incident. We took all sorts of liberties with the rule book. Sometimes small groups of staff had drinking parties at night and off-duty workers came in to join us. Quite often the patients sat up along with us into the early hours. In the mornings the medication trays would slowly spin and shift about under my bilious gaze.

This informal style could lead all too easily to an undoing. One weekend evening I was forced to take an emergency admission. I didn't like the look of him from the start. He was a stocky young man in his twenties, dumped on us as he was supposedly in a crisis. I took one look at his pallid feral features and weaselly eyes and tabbed him for a personality disorder. The resi unit was a fine new playground for him. By six pm on the shift I had already had to return some money that he had extorted out of a gentle Down's Syndrome lad and later still I caught him trying to set off a fire extinguisher. I could see him calculating how far he could push me.

All seemed to have quietened by two am. I began to do my rounds along the hushed carpeted corridors. At each room I'd inch the door open a bit and peek in. Annabel's room was on the last corridor. She was one of my favourites. Only seventeen, with a scoliosed spine and a cute, rubbery little face. She was permanently in a wheel-chair and she had suture scars running up her thin chest like a zipper line from a heart op. She used to clap her hands with pleasure whenever she saw me and I in turn liked to make a fuss of her. As I neared her room I could heard this meaty rhythmic sound. *Thunk! Thunk!* I pushed the door open and the sound grew louder. I could make out in the dim light the new admission sitting astride her chest as she lay in bed. His trousers were undone and his genitals were flopping about near her face. The noise I had heard was him methodically slap-ping at her head and chest. I pulled him off by the back of his collar and dumped him onto the floor. He hitched up his trousers, eyeballed me truculently then lunged at me. I wrestled him out into the corridor. He continued to take round-armed swings at me. The thing that really made me angry was the shameless and calculating way he was doing it. He seemed to think he could get away with anything. I can still visualise his polecat face in that dim corridor. I think he was smiling.

I lost all pretence at professionalism and instinctively punched him hard. It connected on the chin with a crisp clopping sound. He fell instantly and silently and lay on his back in the corridor. I checked to see if he was still breathing. Mercifully, he seemed to be alright and began to stir. I dragged him down the corridor to his room and stuffed him on his bed. His eyes were open, just looking at me. I hurried to see Annabel. She had red marks on her chest and face but seemed to be OK. She babbled quietly to me. I really didn't know what the hell I was going to do and various wild options flared in my head. I went back into his room. He rubbed his face and shrank back when he saw me. I said, "Am I getting any more trouble from you tonight?" He shook his head. In the morning I gave him bus money and discharged him.

Annabel seemed to get over the events of the night. There was no point in warning the authorities about his risks to the vulnerable. His file was full of reports of similar behaviour anyway. My risk to the patients was another thing. I had come close to a professional disaster.

I saw that same problematic abuser some ten years later. It was at a conference about peer support for mental health sufferers. He had become a patient advocate. He even gave a little talk about how he supported people in distress. I dread to think what he was actually doing with them. I'm sure he recognised me. He delivered a lingering varminty stare at me across the crowded room. We were both locked in our secret. I never would again behave as instinctively at work. Perhaps that incident was my farewell to youth. The tiger springs in the new year, he is eating us up but we know it not.

I took less heroic risks after that and somehow also the passionate involvement with the patients grew less intense. That was the negative trade off. At least I would never resemble my more automaton-like colleagues who really put nothing of themselves into their work. I used to think that the patients longed to know us as human beings. I once was assessing a suicidal patient with a consultant psychiatrist whom I respected. The despairing patient said, "Don't you professionals ever realise what depression really feels like?" The consultant replied, "Yes, I have days when I am infinitely sad and it feels as if nothing can mend it." I really thought well of my colleague for saying that.

There were workers right through my career who went the opposite way. Gerry was one such. His poisonous legacy endures and I still find myself brooding about what he did even though so many years have passed. I first met him at a day centre and he became a sort of mentor. He was a sparkling and engaging personality who gave me unstinting support. I counted him a friend as well as a colleague. He was a chunky, middle-aged ex-RAF man with strong square hands. He usually wore short-sleeved shirts summer and winter, with a pack of Consulates usually showing in the top pocket. He always seemed wreathed in a pepperminty menthol vapour. Someone once pasted the advertising slogan "Cool as a mountain stream" on his staff locker door and that did seem to sum up his aura. He was energetic and fiercely intelligent. He could tune car engines and programme computers. He was a glider champion, dance instructor and was fluent in sign language. He bubbled with ideas and schemes about how we could improve our work.

Some people found his intensity almost unbearable but I enjoyed his company and his quirky generosity. He seemed to have a warm and approachable presence, yet had I been more alert I would have seen other things: the way he cultivated the female clients to sit next to him all the time, his long unexplained absences hidden away in their rooms, how he spent hours dabbing on hair tint in the staff toilets, the way that conversations always came back to the same topic — himself.

Gerry was on opposite night shifts to me and the clients always asked, "Who is on tonight? Is it Gerry who is on?" I thought that this was just a reflection of their small institutionalised world but I should have seen something else in their eyes. I had been away from work on a training course and returned to find Gerry gone and an agency worker doing his shifts. No one would tell me why he had been removed. Eventually a senior manager told me over the phone that there had been "irregularities of conduct".

The truth leaked out gradually over the next months that Gerry had apparently been systematically sexually abusing the female residents. Thus every night when I handed on the shift to him and talked of the patients and he'd noted it all down he had actually been planning quite other activities. The wrenching betrayal brought a great doubt to my mind about the nature of all care-giving. I began to wonder if there was not a deep aggression lurking at the heart of seemingly altruistic acts. The mechanism for Gerry perhaps was that he visited harm on the patients out of thwarted disappointment that they could never manifest the improvement that he imagined they should be making. They had to be good for something to him. We will never know, for there was to be no coming to account. There was no legal process as far as I was aware. He could easily have just gone on to work somewhere else. The patients were all shifted to other units. Ever after I have wondered where he went and how he lived with it. There was nothing to be done. In those days that was the way it was handled.

There were quite a few others like Gerry in the ensuing years. Often it was the most magnetic, charming and amusing workers who ended up doing something untoward to the patients. Usually you would only hear about it after they had disappeared. The harm they visited was varied: rubbing up too close to the patients, male staff grooming females and vice versa, romantic affairs with patients — even having children by them, over-enthusiastic restraints, cruel and unusual punishments, selling drugs and alcohol to the patients, neglect, falsifying records, stealing from them, selling stories to the press. Staff were not even safe from each other. Many were the grievances and problems between them. I once had to deliver a reprimand to a senior medical registrar, to his great fury and embarrassment. He had been pestering the more nubile nurses in my team.

Once I had lost the supple confusions of youth, I evolved my own code on how to treat the patients. I became much more careful, having seen the crimes of others. Perhaps I shaped this firm stance because I did not trust my own motivations. I certainly didn't want deaths on my watch. I had seen colleagues torment themselves over suicides. I became over-vigilant, burning extra work time to see that everything was done right. Guilty, fearful thoughts stalked me that I had not done enough for patients. I had a horror of contemplating suffering in other human beings deriving from my own hurt roots. I seemed never to be able to do enough. I worked insanely long hours to make sure I had no souls on my conscience. I did not trust many of my staff and spent my days checking on the quality of what they did while having to do extra to catch up on my own work. I went over their reports and risk assessments. I made sure that they had actually made the visits to patients that they said they had. I asked patients how they had been treated. I checked that mistakes were not made, that risks were properly weighed and all safeguards in place. I no longer believed in luck and gradually I shaped a grimmer responsibility of care.

It was not just the potentially abusive ones that had to be watched. I had found that overly compassionate staff could do harm. The ones who thought patients had the right to do anything they liked, allowing them to starve or self-neglect in suffocating squalor in the name of human rights. I had learned that it was kinder to be firm. This had been taught me by incidents such as when we were called to see a young woman who had become disturbed in an inner city GP's surgery. We had made our decision to section her and an ambulance was backed up to receive her. I noticed her staring up at the sky through the wispy veils of hair that fell over her face as we took her out. I ushered her on board the ambulance then went outside to complete the necessary paperwork, shutting the vehicle back door behind me. She pleaded with me to keep the door open. She was afraid of confinement, she had said, and wanted to see the sunlit world for as long as possible. I weakly agreed. As my attention was distracted she burst out from the back of the vehicle and made a dash through heavy traffic before being run over by a light truck. She was lucky to get away with a fractured tib and fib, but I had learned a deeper lesson.

I also began to understand that we sought out the work in an attempt to heal the wounds within ourselves. There were obvious examples of this all around in the staff rooms — for example, it was striking how many psychotherapy staff had disorders of the eye. There was no end of wonk-eyed therapists whose gaze went north and south at the same time. Heaven knows what the patients made of it. It made me wonder what went on in those rooms where the therapist was supposed to be the mirror of the patients' perceptions and misperceptions and where the direction of the gaze, inward and outward, was a key factor in the helping process. It seemed obvious to me that those strabismic therapists were seducing their own hurts within the contrived love of the therapy rooms. Love so often is a giving of what you haven't got in order to fill a gap. Those poor old boss-eyed therapists were all too obvious yet the real wounded healers were cautious and circumspect like me.

We understood the exquisite pain of knowing how everything is empty and can never be filled right up. We were diligent and over-performing at work. We were often outwardly confident, even formidable clinicians, but inwardly we were actually lonely, avoidant, frightened and miserable. We knew that we needed help but we had become too discriminating to be able to accept it. I continued like that for ten critical years. I was wrapped in a rescue fantasy for my patients that was exhausting but at least it seemed to give me purpose. I have a strange nostalgia for those times now. Caring like that was, at heart, an erotic process. There was a perverse enjoyment in struggling so painfully to heal others in order to avoid dealing with the troubled inferno of one's own being.

I see now that I eventually began to try to cut the knot of my dangerous passion for my patients. I began to change my client group and clinical interests. I had started to understand the mechanism that fuels aggression to the patient. The illusion that we think we know what the other wants or needs which breeds a dislike of the patient who will not conform to our notions of recovery. I solved it by beginning to work with patients that I hated — killers, sex offenders, police work, high risk cases, child tormentors. I began to shift from the principle of *primum non nocere* — firstly do no harm — to the one of *primum processi* — act first, debate later. Sorting out the mess, binding the dangerous patient, preventing him from doing harm to others. That became my speciality. I became known as an infallible and grim clinician. I was reluctant to let anyone out of secure care. So conservative did I become that when I completed independent reports for solicitors' fees — a lucrative sideline for forensic staff — I would never argue for increased liberty. I soon lost the business. After the knowledge that I had accumulated I could give no forgiveness to myself or to patients. I had lost the beauty of my passion for them and had become fearful and constantly pissed-off. And after a while I could not bear even being a jailer.

The last few cases tipped me over the edge. There was one who seemed to exemplify my mood. He was a young man, a student who had gone suddenly mad in the streets. He had kicked and punched at a queue of people by a cash machine then had frenziedly beat his fists against a passing taxi. We did not know what had caused it: a flash flood psychosis maybe, or a drug trip gone wrong. The police holding tanks consisted of a row of brightly lit perspex cabins facing the custody desk. Each illuminated box contained a detainee. They all took up different poses showing despair, anger, resignation — whatever pertained to them. It reminded me of that Celebrity Squares TV game show of my youth.

My fellow, the arrested student, vibrated with barely suppressed violence. I had to interview him but didn't really want to get close to him. He had a pleasant face with thick blond hair which had become furrowed up on top of his head like a crest. His suntanned sinewy tennis player's arms were covered in thin scratches. He had bloody swollen knuckles and strong-looking pincer fingers. He stood in the narrow space jiggling his legs and

34

staring balefully out at the custody staff. They edged the door open. It was like getting into a lift with a bull. I knew he could hurt me.

I swiftly went through the interview, keeping my voice low, not facing him, pitching it light, trying to show I was on his side. He had eyes like ones I had once seen on a monitor lizard in a vivarium, an intense glassy green freckled with tiny black dots. They showed no human contact at all. He jetted out words in a torrent of fury. He didn't know why he was here. It was them. They did it. He jabbed a thumb at the custody staff. Two stood at the half-open door with gloves and helmets on. I wondered if they had laid a bet as to what part of my anatomy he was going to grab first. He kept on speaking in jabbing bursts. He was OK, just wanted to go, wanted to show them something. He slammed the heel of his palm against the perspex with a boom. I knew if I stayed seconds longer he would jump on me.

We eventually took him up to the ward in a police van with a heavy escort. He really began to kick-off then. He crashed a fist against the side of the vehicle during the journey and broke his wrist. This did not slow him and he had three pairs of cuffs on him as we took him up the stairs, half carrying him at every step. He kept bucking and thrashing then grinding out a refrain directed at the men carrying him.

"I'm going to fuck you up, Mr Police Man, just let me go, just let me go and I'll fuck you up. Let me go..." The stairs were long and the repeated threats irritated me immensely. I finally turned on him and roared at him to shut it. Told him to stop abusing us. Didn't he know we were trying to help him? A brittle silence held for a moment. He glared up at me and the police paused in lugging him and looked at me curiously. We reached the intensive care ward, put him into a restraint cell and arranged for sedation so that we could treat his fracture injury. I watched him rubbing his bent wrist and pacing around back and forth on the soft flooring. I had seen thousands of disturbed patients over the years but he just seemed to possess an unfathomable otherness that utterly repelled me. He'd eventually wake from the madness and go back to being an ordinary inoffensive person, with family, friends and lovers. I think it was the animal vigour of his unruly craziness that so undid me. It was probably then, watching him reel about in that restraint room as the ward staff chatted and made cups of tea beside me, that I decided to quit mental health altogether. I had dried out like firewood left too long in the shed. To love one's neighbour as yourself was too cruel an injunction. I was done with it. In the vacant places I would build with new bricks.

# The Cure

Someone had screwed up in medical records. There was an unholy stink. It just couldn't be possible. They had forgotten to renew Brandy's section after the required three years. It had lapsed by two fatal days and absolutely nothing at all could be done about it. All the patients had to be sectioned just like all prisoners had to be remanded or convicted to remain in gaol. Medical records still hadn't been fully computerised. They had relied on manual lists and a new clerk had forgotten to put forward the name for renewal. That, or her file had just slipped down somewhere. Whatever the reason, the head of that department wouldn't be with us for long, that was for sure. The Medical

Director was apoplectic. This simply could not happen in a high security hospital. There could be parliamentary questions about it. If the press got hold of it then that would be the end. The whole thing made a mockery of the hospital as a key engine of control. The great Edwardian façade of the place remained the same; the thick perimeter fence was not breached, yet inside there were frantic last minute activities.

An emergency tribunal was held. Mr White from Evans, Pitkin and White had his moment of victory. He had represented patients in a thousand hopeless tribunal appeals but this one had been given him on a plate. He paced in front of the tribunal members, a scrawny bantam in his dandruff-speckled black suit. He argued that the only way that his client could be retained in the hospital was if she was re-sectioned altogether. To be assessed for a new section she had to show fresh evidence of mental disorder and risk to others. That was the immutable process of the legislation.

Brandy showed no such deterioration. Indeed she seemed pleasant and cooperative. She smiled like a shark at the tribunal members. Her behaviour had been exemplary. Therefore there could be no assessment. One ward nurse muttered to me, "Our Brandy's had a miracle cure!" The Trust lawyers summoned a barrister to argue their case. He pored over the legal precedents and racked up a big bill for the health service but the truth remained the same: she had to be released and straight away at that. Mr White muttered about *habeas corpus* and the Court of Human Rights unless action was taken immediately. The tribunal reluctantly agreed. Brandy would leave the next day. They took her out from HDU — the high dependency lock down where the severe cases were kept for special handling. Back on the main ward the other female patients stared at her triumphal return with awe.

It would have been bad for the hospital if any patient had to be released so unexpectedly, but it was somehow far worse that it was Brandy. She was a horror and a scourge. Corpulent and massively aggressive, her speciality was running at staff down the corridors and flattening them with her weight. That or raking them with her filthy finger nails that she kept long and packed with shit for the purpose. She'd put ten main ward staff on sick leave before they had contained her in HDU. They had managed her there only by going into her cell with shields. One staff member used to feed her through a gap in the shield wall. Even then she had still played them up. She'd given herself toxic shock syndrome by thrusting items up her private parts. She had flicked clots of her bodily filth at staff whenever they let their guard drop. She had got even fatter in HDU, her hair had grown long and untended and had felted into dreadlocked clumps. Her features always reminded me of the Medusa in that old 1980's film, *The Clash of the Titans*. A greenish dead-looking face with terrible stony eyes.

I saw her on one of her rampages once. A great torpedo-like shape in a tracksuit with her massive hair wagging. She'd come running silently down the corridor, side-stepped me, then pounded into a female staff member.

We can imagine the childhood tortures that contributed to her becoming so monstrous. All I can remember from the file was something about her being fed from a dog bowl when she was young. It was a personality deformation in her case rather than frank mental illness. I remembered when she had been admitted to an acute ward in the city long before as a teenager. She used to lounge about shouting at staff in a loud hoarse voice. Weeks, months passed and she never shifted. No-one could move her on. Whenever they tried to discharge her she had made threats or stabbed and poked at herself causing injury. Every intervention was tried: antipsychotic meds, cognitive behavioural work, psychodynamic therapy. The clinicians just broke their teeth on her. Brandy got steadily worse: hitting staff, sticking fingers in light sockets, abusing other patients. She kept getting moved on into deeper and deeper levels of security. All the way to maximum where there were seemingly no more choices left.

She walked down the hospital steps in the metallic light of an early December afternoon. Her meds had been stopped days before at her request and I imagined the consequences of all that serotonin draining out of her synapses. She went through the perimeter gates, the security staff just staring out at her behind their glass cubicles. Her solicitor had offered her a lift but she had refused. Nor would she say where she was going. The cameras swivelled, watching her last steps on hospital ground. A large lady in a down jacket with big hair paddling down the long hospital drive to the bus stop. We followed at a distance in the hospital Mercedes with its smoked windows. An unmarked police car also crept along behind. The radio snorted and clicked as observing staff reported in. It was quite cramped in the Merc. There were, besides the driver, a medic, the head of security and two burly nurses in case shit kicked off. I was there to sign off the section papers if they were needed.

We cruised along in a little convoy the whole seven miles to the nearest town. The back of the bus advertised special curry nights at the Shalimar Restaurant. Squads of rooks at the field margins flittered up as we passed. Brandy remained a dark unmoving shape glimpsed briefly as the bus made its turns. It decanted at a terminus next to a shabby precinct in the quietly dying little English market town. Brandy waddled down the steps and we could see her gazing about. This would be the first time she was out on her own in public in ten or fifteen years. We wound the windows down and watched her in the failing light. She shambled past the Spar shop, a big figure against the illuminated glass. Then past Planet Pizza and a body treatment place. She stopped by the Methodist Church. A few shoppers straggled by without noticing her.

"What's she doing now?" said Head of Security. One of his men had a small pair of binoculars.

"She is next to a family sitting on a bench."

"Not kids," groaned the Head. We could make her out staring down at a couple with their Staffie and a little girl with red felt Christmas antlers attached to her head. I guessed that Brandy had not seen a child or an animal in all her hospital time.

"She's on the move again." We cruised slowly down the High Street following her as she drifted among all the Christmas shoppers. A chill breeze shifted the meagre council decorations, stylised snowflakes hanging on wires. Stacked Christmas trees, enmeshed in nets, lined the shop fronts. A charity emporium had strewn white cotton wool snow on the goods to make them look seasonal. We saw Brandy flinch as a truck ground past. She must have been used to the muffled noises of lock-down these past years. Opalescent light dripped in mauve and red dots from a display in an amusements arcade. *"Feel the heat — take your bingo slot now"* exhorted the sign outside. Brandy slid on, past that, past the exercise dancing adverts and the Christmas drinks special offers. For a moment I had a strange feeling that Brandy was going to make it. It would be like a sort of Christmas truce, a kind of miracle and she'd get free of us and just disappear into the indifferent flow of humanity. Then she wasn't there.

"Find her!" snapped the H.O.S. One of the nurses got out to look for her, joining the other one that had followed her on foot since the bus station.

The radio sputtered. "It's OK, she's gone into a corner shop."

Brandy came back out into our view. She was quite close. She'd bought a coke and a big chocolate bar, a double Twix. She stood eating, limned in the doorway. Nearby was the town Christmas tree, a lopsided Norway spruce contained behind crash barriers. It had a sound system buried in it somewhere that played carols. Brandy took a long time eating her choc bar. She seemed to be looking into a shop window for Prima Donna Lingerie. The mannequins wore red silky exotic underwear. There was sign that read, "Be a Santa baby."

Brandy leaned down and put the coke can at her feet. Her face illuminated for a moment as she lit a fag. She must have bought them in the shop. She wouldn't have been able to do that for years either, after the ban on smoking in hospitals a while back. Her shape barely moved against the brightly-lit shop front. Shoppers kept pouring past her. We could see the fag end glowing as she pulled on it.

"She's moving," came the radio report. She took a pace, flicked the butt away and that thicket of hair bobbed as she picked up her drink again. We watched her arm swing back, *Kerchang!*

She threw the full can right into the lingerie shop window. The glass frosted over with cracks and a bell started ringing. Head of Security said, "Thank Heavens. Let's pick her up." The radio sparked into life and the police car nosed out, blue lights jigging. We could still see Brandy walking away like a drunk. She zigzagged, stopped dead. The shoppers moved around her. She marked time, then her legs gave way and she sat down in the road waiting for us to come.

# The Rescue

I liked to take on the hopeless cases, the heart-sinkers, the personality disorders, the ones whom no one else would go near. I'm not sure why. Maybe I just felt somehow closer to those unlikable, incurable ones than to the more manageable clients. My psychotherapy supervisor once observed that she saw in me someone trying to give the care to others that I craved for myself. I think that I just got a kick out of rescuing people. It was my chance to be a hero which my cowardice had prevented me from enacting in other more conventional ways. Somehow, dealing with those problem patients built up my self-esteem. There was a hubris there, an arrogant assumption that I alone could cope with them. Over the years though, those difficult cases became a way to punish the self. The no-hopers began to grind me down and there were some that threatened to undo me altogether. There were times when Marie seemed to be one such.

She had been born to a Caribbean man, a lifer doing time for murder. Her mother was a scary, hard-faced slattern, a white woman with a coarse grating voice who shouted at the social workers that came looking for her daughter. Rumour had it that she had worked as a prossie for years down those bleak inner city terraces. The family lived in a squalid warren of nineteenth century back-to-backs, an area the council had lacked the will to improve.

Marie had sprung from those neglected streets and was shaped by a monstrously abusive family. She was a young woman when I first met her. Late twenties, but it was hard to say. She always looked a fright with her untended afro, brightly coloured plastic clips thrust into its thickets. She had thin, scarred, bare legs with knock knees. She seemed like a child wearing baggy adult clothes all flapping about her narrow frame. Her feet were usually thrust into over-large charity shop shoes. She scraped and scuffed her way along and seemed often to be tottering forward as if about to overbalance. Her hands were forever anxiously rubbing or picking at her face while her small bewildered eyes darted hither and thither. She spoke through her nose like someone with a cleft palate, her raspy voice ascending to an ear-splitting shriek once she was agitated, which was quite often. Her face could have been attractive but was usually alcohol-bloated, tear-stained and wracked with terror or rage. Her coppery skin was flecked with scars where she had stabbed and poked at herself with knives, blades, objects of all sorts. Yes, she was a mess. It was a car crash of a life. She never had any money. Always shuffling to the offie to haggle for credit from the wary Asian proprietors. Half-cut and rowing with the neighbours or on the run from pitiless men who had scented her vulnerability like hyenas around a crippled animal. All her life people had either taken advantage or given up on her.

I had got involved as child care could not manage and they had requested a mental health opinion. Marie was the terror of the Child Care Services. She had a little boy called Perry, a product of some long-dissolved relationship. There was a constant worry that she was not a fit mother, and by any measure she probably wasn't. I had been hauled in as a last option to assess her to see if she could improve with treatment. She had a virulent hatred of social services and there were many stories about the unpleasant things that happened to workers who had called at her door. She had never cooperated with the authorities and despite her reeling chaos she had somehow beaten them off for a long time. She seemed to have rebuffed them with a combination of innate cunning and by grinding them down with her sustained hostility. The council had begun legal moves to take Perry away permanently. I think they hoped that I would section her and carry her off to a locked ward and then everything could just be tidied up. After going through her thick files, I rang her family doctor to get the latest view.

"What can you do with her? I have run out of ideas long ago," the GP had said. "All I do is inject her with a contraceptive so at least she can't have any more children."

So I, a middle-aged, burnt-out mental health worker in a jacket and tie, came calling on Marie. The auguries were not good that I would get on any better than the others. I arrived early. All the dogs along the terrace had seemed to scent a stranger and set up a frenzied alarm. The kids stopped thumping a football against a wall and stood watching me with closed rigid faces. Her battered door opened a crack and I could make out a single eye burning a high voltage stare.

"Yeah?"

I explained that I was there to see if I could help, no, I was not Child Care. The door opened a bit, "You'd betta come in," she said.

She made an exception with me for some unfathomable reason. Her front room was bleak and bare. It had an austere look to it but was not as messy as I had anticipated. Although the plaster walls had lots of dints and holes from hurled objects, her few possessions were arranged in an orderly way and rows of her smalls were drying in front of the single gas fire. Perry appeared, a shy wraith of a child, flitting through the chilly house. I patted him on the head and gave him a sweet. You were not supposed to do that sort of thing but I did not care much for orthodoxy. Marie poured out her troubles in a gabbling torrent. We were interrupted when the Child Care social workers called. They were rebuffed savagely at the door.

"I've got someone here already. That's enough. You lot can fok off. You can gerrat of it."

So it started. I saw Marie weekly for six years in the end.

The work was awful. Marie dragged me in her chaotic wake through Child Care offices, courts, hospital casualty units, solicitors' offices and detox facilities. When she was completely drunk and wild I'd carry Perry away to his grandmother's house. Marie tested me to the limit, once holding a big paring knife on me, prodding the point into my chest. The end of the blade caught on a shirt button and I could feel it press onto my breast bone as she slurred out, "I want you to feel my pain. I want you to feel it. Feel how I'm hurting." Somehow I never believed she would actually harm me, although occasionally I had to evade her. Once I had to leap out of her kitchen window to get away after she had locked me into her house and squirted lighter fuel over me, herself and the whole room. She kept flicking her lighter but it wouldn't take.

"I can't even burn meself," she had sobbed.

There were long, tear-sodden accounts of her childhood horrors. Of mum's male customers being ushered into her bedroom at night. Of the unpredictable rages and grasping hands of her psychopathic father. Of the day when, desperately looking for something to eat, she had found a dead baby wrapped tightly in cellophane in the bottom of a cupboard. Her present life also tormented her, crises, money troubles, lost benefit cheques, cruelties from men skulking in the shadows. She would loll on her sofa while reeling out the horrible stories and at the same time pressing razor blades to her neck or arms. Her velvety blood kept welling up until I prised the blades out of her fingers.

During the very bad times she would take overdoses. She did this maybe five or six times severely enough to call an ambulance. She was as incompetent at poisoning herself as she was at most other things. I'd usually bring some clothing for her to the hospital. The ward would be thick with resentment towards her as they were busy enough with patients who were really ill. She'd change in the toilets and come scuffing out in her ill-fitting shoes.

"Bastards!" she'd yell as a parting shot.

Often we would have to pause outside as she retched violently into the hospital shrubberies.

I never ceased to wonder at her salamander ability to withstand the fires of her own excesses. I saw my main function as preventing her from dying. Sometimes this seemed a quixotic enterprise, given her furious destructiveness. Gradually, I began to marvel at her ability to survive and I secretly smiled at her triumphs over the dead hand of authority. She also began hesitantly to take some of my advice. A turning point came when I had cajoled and pressured her to go to an alcohol-rehab unit. This was a huge thing for her to do. The place was twenty miles away and required a week's stay. She had never travelled more than a mile or so from her corner of the world except for one school day trip years before. Perry went off to his grandma's uncertain clutches and after many false starts and delays we set forth. Things seemed to be going alright with Marie uncharacteristically silent, staring intently at cows and trees and green vistas when passing motorists began to hoot and flash at me.

"What is wrong?" asked Marie, I realised that I was trailing a plume of smoke out the back of my old Renault. We came to a rapid halt and I hauled Marie out although she moaned and struggled. We then stood shivering in a whipping February wind on the side of a busy road as the conflagration took hold and consumed the car entirely in a fierce orange blaze. I found out later that a leaking fuel pump had been dripping onto a hot exhaust. The fire crew gave us a ride back in their tender and her neighbours gaped in amazement as we rolled down her street in the big red machine. As she wobbled out on her thin legs Marie said to me, "That's the last time I ever go anywhere with you again!" Then she giggled, doubling over in merriment. I'd never seen her laugh before.

It was hard to see progress and if you got too comfortable she could take you back down to the bottom again. Over time the self-harming gradually diminished and her drinking slowed although she never did get to rehab. She started taking Perry to school and even bought him a puppy for company. She could still make my heart bump sometimes with her ructions and upsets, and shaken Child Care workers would complain to me about their maulings at her hands, but life by any measure got a little better. I still visited regularly but had to be on my guard. Like the day I found that she had picked up some live pistol ammo off the street (it was that sort of neighbourhood) and had stored the bullets on top of her gas fire as ornaments. There was also the afternoon that I came round, found the door open and heard her calling me from the second floor of her house. I entered an upstairs room to find her lying naked on her bed, her arms cradled behind her head.

"What are you doing, Marie?" I had said.

"I'll be down in a minute," is all that she replied. We never discussed the incident. I suppose it was a kind of test. I could never forget the strange beauty of that scarred body.

Inevitably the time came for me to move to another job. I put off saying anything about it to the last moment. I was going to work at a hospital forty miles away. Her face folded in sadness when I finally told her, but there were no scenes or upsets. I spouted the usual positive things about how well she had done and how she would cope alright in the future. Even her hard mother came down on my last visit, just nodding to me when I bid her goodbye. Marie said, "Take me to the offie a last time. I'll really need a drink now." We rode quietly together in the car. I noticed she had put on a bit of green eye shadow. When I dropped her off she said, "Here, I've bought you something," and handed me a little parcel wrapped in tissue. It contained a tiny vintage lead model soldier, she must have bought it from the corner junk shop. A battered miniature marching figure.

"Think of me sometimes," she said, kissed me on the cheek then scuttled away.

I went on with my career. I kept her little marching figure on my study bookshelves and sent her cards at Christmas with a £20 note inside for a few years. A colleague from my old team eventually told me that he thought she had moved away.

Ten years later I had left clinical practice behind and now inhabited a desk job and dealt with abstract issues. I was addressing a group of local health staff on policy matters. I had launched into my talk when my address was interrupted by an insistent hammering sound. Heads in the audience turned towards the door. There was a hatch-like window and I could just make out a face and a waving hand. Instinctively, I responded to the call and left the podium like a sleep-walker. The audience rustled and whispered in my wake.

It was Marie standing in the doorway looking well, smartly turned out, her face glowing healthily and her eyes were clear.

"Thought it was yer," she said, "I was here to see my doctor. I live nearby. I saw yer go in. Ages and ages I waited. Couldn't wait any longer. Sorry about the banging."

We embraced awkwardly.

"You look well," I ventured.

"Yes, I'm not bad. I've still got a lot of problems though. I'd like to talk to yer."

"It's wonderful to see you," I stammered out lamely, "But I must go back in to my meeting."

"Well, yer look the same. Jus the same," she said, "But if yer have ter go. Here..." She handed me a piece of paper on which she had written her address in a wobbly hand. It had probably taken her ages to write it.

I went back to the speaker's dais with the audience craning to see who it was.

"Sorry about that. Someone I'd not seen for years," I said, then I completed my talk on statutory developments in healthcare.

She was gone by the time we all came out. It was strange to see an older Marie, so much more poised than I remembered her. Sometimes you would rather think of people you are fond of in caricature as if that somehow preserves them from change and loss. I walked back to my car in the rain and looked at the crumpled piece of paper where she had so carefully written down her address. I shredded it and let it fall to the wet pavement and watched the fragments wash away. I knew I could not see her. Better for her to be free of me. All those years I thought I had been rescuing her, she had been really rescuing me.

# The Practice
# of Deliverance

When did Margie ask me to arrange for an exorcism? Probably when she realised my own ability to rid her of her demons had manifestly failed. It came as a shock though. She wasn't evidently religious. A washed-out blonde, in her forties with a prematurely seamed face, she did not seem to have any serious interests. I usually found her flipping through gossip magazines with lurid covers or polishing her gaudy nails. She lived in a line of tenement houses each guarded by rows of uneven iron railings sawn off at the bases like stumps of rotten teeth. She had a little girl called Shaunice, no father in sight. The child liked to wave her plump café-au-lait arms at me in greeting when I visited. I always found her in the same place, sat in front of a giant TV wreathed in her mother's fag smoke. Margie lived off benefits but probably had other sources of income, the precise nature of which I could never quite work out. Her house seemed always full of new appliances. She also kept adding to a collection of dolls in national costume, all ranked in a line with staring porcelain faces. I had been called in to help her pervasive low mood and anxiety. Life was pressing her down and antidepressants were not working. I had already been visiting for six months but her problems seemed intractable. She complained a lot about feeling low and panicky but never actually looked distressed. There was an odd blankness about her.

Then the psychic events began to occur. They were strange happenings, though not in themselves seemingly very significant. One could say that they were even a bit ridiculous, although Margie evidently viewed them in a serious light. Firstly, she complained that Jo-Jo — her budgie — had been hurled bodily in his cage across the sitting room by some invisible force. She showed me some feathers on the carpet as an aftermath, and an agitated-looking bird. I asked her if she had actually seen the incident, but no, she had just heard the crash of the cage and the shrieking of the inhabitant. She also reported that something made noises in her bedroom while she was in the bath. It rattled drawers and seemed to swing on door handles and light fittings. Whenever she rushed into the room to check what was happening there would be nothing to see. Just a furtive silence and a slightly vibrating lamp shade.

I tried rational explanations for the phenomena but Margie would not accept them. The big event occurred one morning when I received a panicky call to come round at once. I found her pacing in her back garden. She said that a plant pot had been extracted from her house by supernatural means, had made its way across her back garden and had then been hurled onto the bonnet of a neighbour's car. I inspected the scene and indeed found the remains of an uprooted schefflera plant lying on top of an old VW Golf. Blobs of compost and shreds of plant also clung to a nearby fence as if an entity had leaped away over the gardens to do mischief elsewhere. Now would I believe her? She demanded. Her tone was triumphant. I assumed that she had done the damage herself.

I questioned her as to why a malignant spirit might be afflicting her. Was the trouble residing in the fabric of the house or was it within her did she think? She could give me no answer and remained strangely vacant and resistant to interpretation. All I could get from her was a sense of oppression, lurking malaise, bad hoodoo. It might all have been to do with the large amount of heavy grade skunk she smoked with the young neighbourhood Rastas. I used to find them all together sometimes on my visits. These dudes had thick braids falling to their shoulders giving them a hunched appearance. They would stare at me in heavy hostile silence when I arrived with my attaché case. Margie always looked unruffled. She would make excuses, Shaunice would give me a wave and I'd be shown out and asked to come again another time.

It was always exorcism that she insisted on whenever she saw me. Week after week she kept saying that this was what was needed to turn her life round and get rid of the rooted sorrows that were afflicting her. I tried to explore why she was externalising everything and encouraged her to control issues herself. A flicker of annoyance would appear then: did I want her to end up like Jo-Jo, hurled to the ground by a malignant presence? I countered by doggedly questioning what exorcism really meant to her.

"I want rid. Don't you understand?"she'd whine. Still I tried to probe. She hadn't got an idea about exorcism from church because she never went there. There was a crucifix among the jumble of gold chains around her thin perma-tanned neck but I had presumed that that was just a ghetto-style accoutrement. She denied that anyone else had put the idea into her head. Had she been seen casting out demons in horror films? Linda Blair grunting and head spinning? She just shrugged. No, she didn't watch that sort of thing. She seemed to know of it by other means. Some odd atavistic idea that had occurred to her and would not leave. I also began to think that if I helped this casting-out to happen then it might in itself be more helpful to her than all my visits and packets of tablets. Perhaps it would be more healthy for her to minister to herself in this way and rid herself of the things that weighed upon her heart.

I didn't want to make it too public among my colleagues. There was a secular rationalist orthodoxy at work. Our consultant psychiatrist had once told me that his Sylheti patients were particularly demon-infested.

"In Bangladesh, he who does not believe in the djinn does not believe in the Koran," he said only half-jokingly. I knew that electro-convulsive therapy, which was shunned with horror by most of the population and used by us as the final option for only really bad cases, was extremely popular among his Asian patients. It seems that they all asked for the electric shocks as these were considered the most efficacious for driving out the djinn demons of mental illness.

"Exorcism? Well I suppose if it's patient choice then we should arrange it," said Simon, the hard-bitten charge nurse, after he stopped laughing when I told him about it. "Perhaps it should be put on the NHS treatment menu." He warned me not to enter it in the patient notes though. It wouldn't look good in any enquiry.

Where to start? The local Church of England wouldn't touch it.

"Try the charismatic churches," said one vicar whom I had contacted through the hospital chaplaincy. After several weeks of enquiries a call came back.

"We do not call it exorcism, sir," said a brisk male voice over the phone, "We call it 'the practice of deliverance'." My contact seemed unsurprised when I outlined Margie's problem. I asked if he did this often.

"Oh yes, sir. All the time, we are very busy."

The appointed day came, I was a lot more nervous than Margie. I could just see the headlines: *Mental health worker in exorcism scandal.*

Marge had not prepared especially for the occasion other than putting a cloth over Jo-Jo's cage. Shaunice had been settled closer to the telly and given a large bottle of pop. The exorcists were a two man team. The lead was a neat little fellow bound into a tight suit and hefting a large basalt-coloured Bible. He had a lean lugubrious assistant, like a funeral director, who followed him at two paces and never said a word the whole time. I squirmed inwardly with queasy regret at being involved in it all but I had stepped in so far, like Macbeth, and I thought I had better stay in order to manage any disaster that might occur.

The exorcists were ushered in and refused refreshment. Two dark strangers in Margie's kitchen. They stared at her dolls with disapproval. They had come to do serious business. I had read somewhere that the word exorcism comes from the Greek for 'binding with oaths'. And that is what kept fluttering in my mind, *a binding with oaths*. What have I been bound to? And what would be the consequences?

First the little man sat Margie down and gave her a talk. Her listless vacant eyes barely focussed on him.

"Now, my dear. You have called us here to rid you of the things of the Devil. But it's no good driving demons out if your heart remains impure. Also if you do not believe then they will make their homes here again. Do you understand?"

"Yes," said Margie tonelessly.

"We work by cleansing hearts for Jesus. We do not use priests. We are workers for the Lord. For it says in Luke 10:17, 'I have given you authority to trample on snakes and scorpions and to overcome ALL the power of the enemy.' Now, Marjorie, we find so often that demon possession is caused by rebellion..."

"It's Margie," my client interrupted with surprising asperity.

"Alright, Margie," he said, raising his voice to regain authority, "You already have spirits of infirmity. This good man is trying to help you."

He pointed at me.

"But sometimes you need stronger medicine. Now these spirits can get into you in various ways. By curses or by being inserted. Tell me, my dear," he lowered his tone. "Have you been raped? It can happen like that."

"No, that's always been all voluntary like," replied Margie.

"I see," said head demon chucker and gave a little cough. Margie evidently was not going to be that easy. "You do believe? It will make it worse if you do not believe. And you will lead a good life after? You will renounce temptation and negative living and repent?"

Shaunice stirred and wailed. "Shurrup na," yelled Margie. She broke away to wheel the child's high-chair nearer the telly. "Yes, duck. I do repent," she said tonelessly.

"Very well, we will proceed." The head exorcist began to pace jerkily about the downstairs rooms, sizing the place up. He was very brisk.

"What would you like me to do?" I said meekly.

He looked at me with a prickly gaze. I could tell he thought I was a sceptic.

"You remain seated, sir. Keep a sharp eye," he indicated the back garden under a grey sky. "Demons often fly out, perch on lamp posts and sometimes they dart back in to the house. You keep a good watch."

Then, his Bible open and followed by his lanky sidekick with Margie bringing up the rear, he commenced marching through the rooms up and down stairs shouting in a stentorian voice,

IN THE NAME OF JEESAS
I bind you.

IN THE NAME OF JEESAS
I command you to go quietly.

IN THE NAME OF JEESAS
I expel you.

IN THE NAME OF JEESAS
I command you never to return.

IN JESAAS' NAME
I close all doors that allowed you entry.

Listening to them, I found my chest knocking in a quick stammer of panic. That authoritative blaring voice seemed to come stamping out alive from a frightening past and I regretted starting the whole business. I willed my breathing to slow and as the minutes passed I stared out at the back garden as they thudded and banged about upstairs.

They came back downstairs and the caster-out went on tiptoe, put his hands on Margie's head and said,

"Jeesas, I adore and praise you for your deliverance of the demon of Margie. Jeesas, I adore and praise you for your deliverance of the demon of Margie." She herself maintained her usual zombie-like expression. The trio then proceeded to the front door. The little man opened and closed the door with a slam while loudly chanting, "Jeesas, I ask You to fill with Your Holy Spirit those empty spots vacated by the demons who left so that when they try to come back there will be no place for them. I close all doors that allowed you entry."

He did the same at the back door and gave that a particularly vigorous slam. The party then advanced towards me.

"Did you see anything, sir?" I was asked.

"No," I replied regretfully.

"The demons may still be inside," said the exorcist grimly. He looked at the ranks of Margie's doll collection with their gleaming pale faces.

"I'd get rid of those, love," he said. "Now, nearly done," he went on and he and his assistant advanced on Margie with his Bible aloft.

"In Jeesas' name heal Margie's spirit of infirmity. Close all spiritual doors opened to demonic activity. When demonic symptoms of depression return in Jeesas' name we firmly reject them. We thank and praise God for what He has done."

Margie, who had been standing like one of her dolls, arms limply to the side with her head tipped over so that her lank blond hair was almost touching the big grainy bible, suddenly started coughing. I thought it was fag deficiency but the deliverance men both smiled triumphantly.

"It's the demons coming out!" called out the lead.

He pressed home his advantage, "Heal Margie," he chanted. "Heal Margie. Heal Margie. It is you, Father in the name of Jeesas, who delivers from the pit and corruption of depression and dark doings. Now say after me..."

He gave his Bible to his assistant and took Margie by the shoulders so that she faced him. She shuffled round like a somnambulist.

"Thank you for becoming a curse on the cross for me, so that I may be freed of all curses that are due to my own sins or the sins of my ancestors. Jeesas. I trust that you will take care of the demons and also take care of me. I resist the devil, in your name, Jeesas. Amen."

Margie murmured in her flat voice, "Take care of the demons and take care of me."

He went to Shaunice who dragged her eyes from the giant screen to stare up at him. "Take care of the demons and take care of this child."

He went past Jo-Jo's shrouded cage.

"Hold on, what is this?" he asked suspiciously.

"It's me budgie," said Margie.

The exorcist exchanged a grim look with his sidekick, "We should pray over this too. Demons inhabit creatures. You have heard of the Gadarene swine?"

"No," said Margie.

"I command you to leave and never return!" he incanted over the cage. All was still within. Jo-Jo, perhaps wisely, kept silence.

At last, all assembled by the front door. Barely ten minutes had elapsed since the beginning of it all. Margie was given a business card,

"If you slip or fall it is better that you confess it once. This is where you can contact us."

Both exorcists shook her hand.

"Be of joy and gratefulness," urged the exorcist. Margie stared back at him like an automaton. I assisted in ushering them out, smiling guiltily. I was relieved it was over and my client not foaming on the floor.

"I'm tired. It takes such a lot out of you," he whispered to me as if we were both in the same business. I began to close the door behind them but he popped his head round for a last time, "Remember it says in John, the Lord comes so that we can have life and have it more abundantly."

Then they were gone. Margie shuffled into the kitchen, there was a pink tinge to her cheeks under her matte brown make-up as if she had been exerting herself.

"Let's have a cup of tea, duck," she said.

I closed the case soon after. I'm not sure how I worded it in the notes. *Signposted to spiritual advisor* or something like that. Her symptoms weren't very much better but she seemed settled and she had certainly stopped complaining. Maybe that ceremony had really released Margie from something that I could not reach. It is strange how old beliefs linger on however shallow the life. I never did see the demons come flying out from Margie's house but looking back, there was a strange alchemy at work in those minutes that I waited during her exorcism. Life, seemingly full of unfulfilment, had gone on. A wagtail skittered on a garage roof, TV aerials vibrated in a chill February breeze, old nappy bags blew over the unkempt turf to snag in the leafless ash stems at the bottom of her garden. That day, like so many, seemingly empty and effaced of meaning, yet all the while trees kept sending deep avid roots down to work furiously in the earth.

# Good Morning, Death

*"Thou knowest I am as valiant as Hercules, but beware instinct.... Instinct is a great matter".*
HENRY IV, PART I, ACT II.

My colleagues had always seen me as being good in an emergency. I kept a cool head and could be relied on in a tight spot. In reality though I had always been frightened. Every day had been a struggle for control. A sort of dread permeated my life. Now everything was coming to pass. How had it started? I wasn't absolutely sure. At first it was just a feeling which had then grown to a nagging thought that wouldn't go away. This had now hardened into an unshakeable belief. I was utterly sure. The day had arrived when I was going to get the chop.

I had woken and the fear had woken with me. I'd slid from the soft shallow prison of vivid dreams. Light was fingering at the curtains and I had watched the clock radio numerals slot round. I had lain on one side, foetal, letting nature have its way. I had just kept on rehearsing in my mind how everything was going to pan out. My mobile phone rang its alarm bell. It was a tinkling harmless little tune but still it packed a punch. Beethoven's *Für Elise*. It gave me a jolt each time it sounded. I wished I hadn't downloaded it. Ha! Should have used Chopin's Prelude Number Two. *Presentiment of Death*. Strange that a sardonic part of me should find it all a bit comically unreal. Laughter was a good pesticide. But still the icy thoughts kept trickling back. The phone alarm rang again. The room lit up with a spectral glow each time it sounded. I got up to prevent a third summons. Sweat down the small of the back. A robin sang lustily outside. That bird would likely survive the day. Took a look from between the curtains. A fissile dawn silvering to bland morning light. The wind scraping the front garden limes this way and that. To see it no more tomorrow. Others will get up and I will not.

Stop that! It was a futile, degrading terror that must be driven back.

Not far away my nemesis would be stirring. The ward usually rose early. They called him "Tiny" but his real name was Devon. Devon Kingdom. He pronounced it "Devanne" in the Jamaican style. Everyone else called him "Tiny" in clumsy irony because he was so monstrously large. 6 foot 4 inches and 280 lbs. Built like a bull. And a badass to go with it.

The trees continued their semaphore. They signalled, "finis, finis" — an aubade. I tried to move on with my morning routines. It was strange how life could be consumed by busy pointless things right up to the end. I went through the fussy, consoling rituals of dressing and of breakfast. Fear dulled everything. I crunched on a little toast. It tasted like burnt paper. That dodgy bicuspid flared a bit. Too late to get it fixed now. I kept on checking the clock. An hour and a half left. Tiny's shadow filled the mind. That lowering shape was a lot clearer than the vaguer metaphysical fear of non-being that had so often afflicted me in the past. *Timor mortis conturbat me.* What did the poet Larkin say to the nurse on his death bed? Yes, the inevitable, "I am going to the inevitable."

I knew what acute fear was like. I had been attacked, stabbed at and set fire to in my career. I'd had to run several times from maniacs. The worst had been on a plane long ago. A jumbo over Miami that had suddenly filled with thick smoke. The fear then was like an electric charge to the heart and entrails. Especially when I heard the first high screaming of the other passengers. In that case it turned out to be a faulty air conditioning unit and all was set right after a sickening five minutes. The nightmare was smoothed away to be replaced by a free whisky all round and apologies over the intercom. But this unreasoning conviction that Tiny was going to really do for me had grown over twelve long hours. After all, who was going to really stop him? I had an image from those videos: *When Animals Attack.* I used to rerun them again and again. Thick implacable necks and twisting great horns as the beasts tossed the Pamplona runners. Tumbling rag dolls under the brute power. My fear today was not like that plane panic. It was a slow sick feeling that had now settled into the glum acceptance of the condemned man.

It was all set. I had to see Tiny that morning. An appointment to sign the section papers. The law dictated that an appropriate assessment had to be made within the proper time limits. That meant meeting him face-to-face. The day before we'd had a confrontation. Devon had been in the restraint room. All padded in blue spongy carpeting. We had tried talking to him, the psychiatrist and me, but Tiny had erupted. He'd rampaged despite the restraints and the posse of staff trying to hold him. He ripped his bulky arm free from their combined grip, pointed at us and had bellowed threats. The doc said timidly, "Do you mean me, Mr Kingdom?"

"Nat yo. Dat backra dere," the huge finger stabbed directly.

"Me gwine 'ave him." Pointing again straight at me.

"Do time for ya! Me waiting for ya! Mash ya up!"

The minders pulled him away and the heavy door slammed. His face still at the armoured window mouthing, "Mash ya!"

Devon and I had form. It went back three years before. I had used a Section 135 warrant of entry to get into his place when he had last gone mad. The police had to use "an enforcer" — a metal device for bashing in the surprisingly strong plastic front door. Tiny's paranoid illness had flared. He'd caked himself in white stuff, possibly dried toothpaste. Tiny had apparently believed it made him invisible to his enemies. He had plunged out of the house once the door had busted, flattening two bulky police at the front of the entry crew in the process. Tiny had made straight to attack me then and I'd had to escape through a line of police shields. Tiny had barrelled about the street half-naked, all smeared in that chalky war paint like some ancient Nubian warrior. I had left my attaché case containing the warrant on the ground. Tiny had jumped up and down on it while the police watched him over their shields.

"At least it's not you he's jumping on, sir," said the superintendent in charge at the time.

Now I was back, exposed to him again. Fate had somehow steered it that I had to get into a room with him and tell him that he was mentally ill and dangerous and was to be detained for six months. Tiny already hated me, and today he was really going to blow his stack. What could I do to change it? Call in sick? Someone else would have to do it and that went against my stubborn, stupid, old-fashioned sense of honour.

Maybe it would be OK. At the worse Tiny would make a grab and the staff would haul him off. Why had I developed that unshakeable notion that Tiny was going to do for me? Once again I tried to rationalise. Still it stuck with me. Unresting and unreasoning. The terrible, barbed certainty that Tiny was going to rend me into pieces.

I stepped to the bathroom to look at my sick doomed face in the mirror. I shat small grey turds like noisome bullets. Washed and shaved and donned the martyr's clean white shirt. Smooth belly adorned by silky little hairs. My body kept on tenderly pulsing away, going through its processes regardless. I dressed carefully. Chose a tie of muted smoky hue. Best to make sure everything was clean. Didn't want any embarrassment if they had to cart me into ED. I no longer smoked but really felt like a fag now.

One, no two — hell, there's three! Grackling away to themselves, tails up, the magpies bounced athletically on the neighbour's front lawn. One for sorrow, two for joy, three for a funeral. I was already down the street and the house had closed its doors to me. It would continue its quiet life very well without me. It was early spring, and the new buds were punching out saying the old year is dead — begin, begin. My footsteps sounded on the pavement. Prognostications were ridiculous, I kept telling himself. Perhaps my cowardly intuitions were all wrong. Maybe everything had been cancelled. Tiny might have become reasonable. Maybe he understood now he had an illness that needed to be treated. Let's all behave rationally and shake each other by the hand.

Slamming of the traffic on the busy main road. All those cars like tumbrels. Faces stared at me through windscreens then whisked past. They had absolutely no notion of the cruel mechanisms of life. It didn't matter how you called it, the deal was shitty. A dead fox was bundled there on the tarmac, its body folded sharply back against itself. I'd looked at it before but now I looked more sharply. The teeth were grinning.

Lined up at the bus stop. Ridiculous to be so disciplined. I kept yawning and dissolving into tears. "*It Could Be You!*" read the advert. Apparently 30% of lottery winners said they had received a prophetic sign of their coming winnings. What about losers then? I had always thought it highly possible one day that a patient was going to kill me. I'd noted the newspaper accounts. One or two mental health workers a year were knocked off. Most of the poor old patients weren't dangerous at all but I seemed to be drawn to the really problematic ones. I knew an OT in a secure unit who had been killed by a screwdriver in her back. There was something about me, despite my cowardice, that flirted with risk. Like those people who go out on seaside promenades whenever there is a big storm. I'd certainly smelt the sour breath of danger in my time. There was Ian D. who quietly informed me that he had a Bowie knife in his rucksack and was contemplating inserting it in me. And that girl in the psychotherapy waiting room who had fastened herself onto me like a bull mastiff, her teeth buried in my thigh. And Mina U. Surprisingly strong in her hijab. She'd taken a pistol in to her appointment. When I removed the weapon from her she lobbed a fire extinguisher straight at my head. And Midge, a body builder with a head injury. Dealing with him was like holding a severed high voltage electricity cable every day. I'd worked with him for six years and never relaxed. I briefly entertained the notion of Midge being pitted against Tiny like Predator vs. Alien. I thought that Tiny would probably win.

There had been so many near misses. It was stupid really to count them up though. You were more likely to get run over by a bus.

The doors duly opened with a hiss of invitation. I took a good look at the other passengers. One should always do that. You never know what you will be going through together. They all looked safe enough but sooner or later everyone will have to get off. There were two miles to travel to the hospital and half an hour left. I tried to see it straight. It was a modern unit — safe, specialist and secure. I'd done it all a hundred times. You just needed to keep away from him. Ask him a few questions then sign the papers. You don't even need to spend time on the clinical details. Just sign it and go. That's it. I needed to get a grip. The bus jolted and Tiny's face wobbled up in my mind's eye. It was like a block carved roughly out of a lump of mahogany.

Somebody had once tried to set fire to Tiny. There was a shiny smear of burnt skin down the right side of his shaved head. The burning had dripped along the side of his face and pulled one eye down. It gave him a malignant lop-sided stare. His mouth was always open as if he was scenting out his victims from some special gland. The hump of trapezoid muscle on top of Tiny's shoulders thrust his head forward giving him a menacing jutting pose. It was no good. I shook myself. My eye followed an elderly male passenger who felt his way with a stick and sat in a seat reserved for the disabled. What had happened to my caring feelings? Tiny was just vulnerable in his own way. He deserved compassion.

How had Tiny got like this? Couldn't something have been done? He was like a giant lethal child. The parents must have had something to do with it. That or rotten genes. There were three Kingdom brothers — all gone to bad. One brother was in jail for rape with trimmings and the other in some sort of secure care. He apparently had a learning disability. Tiny was evidently heading the same way. It was depressing to see how many Caribbeans were on the psychotic wards anyway. I wasn't going to theorise about the reasons for that epidemic. I'd leave it to the researchers. All I knew was that these were not factitious illnesses, created by culturally misunderstanding doctors. These guys were crazy alright, and Tiny when he got going was as mad as a box of frogs. Ah, there was no use speculating now. The spring light rippled across my face although the day outside seemed as white as clay. I could feel the warmth through the glass. The bus tyres made a drubbing sound as they bowled along. The noise sounded like *mutilate mutilate*.

Tiny filled the cramped interview room. The patient was all herded round with staff. There was an unexpected smell of flowery aftershave. Tiny was in a hooded grey top. It had the logo *Champ* across his vast chest. A beanie hat was perched on the back of his conical head. He looked like a boxer in training doing a pre-fight press conference.

"Wh'appen?" said Tiny. His voice was slurry and slow unlike the previous day. All were invited to sit. The chairs and tables were screwed down to prevent them being hurled.

"Nah, I stand," said Tiny. He leaned against a wall, his solid forearms folded in front of him. "What yo have to say to me?"

Now was the time to start. My mouth was dry. I wished I'd brought some water. I kept a tight hold on my rollerball pen. I might be able to stick it in his eyes at a pinch.

"Now, Mr Kingdom, do you understand why you are on the ward?" It was a roundabout way of getting going. Tiny looked puzzled.

"What is it? What yo sayin' to me? When am I leavin'?"

Now we are to it. This is the very nub. I launched into it.

"You are to be detained, Mr Kingdom, Section Three. A six month treatment order. You have the right to appeal against it."

Tiny kept his head down sunk on his chest. You could just see the top of his little watch cap. He then raised his head to glare terribly. His eyes were like black holes jammed in the yellowed sclera.

"A fool? You tink I'm a fool?"

"No, we don't think you are a fool, Mr Kingdom." I was beginning to falter and my voice sounded weak and thin. Now we were for it.

There was a commotion outside the interview room. Alarms sounded and a bleeper kept going off.

"It's a Rapid Response call, an emergency on another ward. We have to go," said the heavy-set team leader. "You will have to step out of here while we sort this out. We can carry this on later."

"No, we are OK here. You go on," I replied.

"Are you sure?" said the team leader.

Heaven knows why I said such a thing. I was always frightened of heights but still kept staring over cliffs to look into the abyss.

What would be would be.

The two of us remained as the posse of staff thundered off down the corridor. We were left alone. Tiny moved, brought his hand up to his face and rubbed his eyes.

"Deetentshan is it, sah?" he said with a sigh. He made to sit down. He seemed too big for the chair. He put his head in his hands.

"Men all grind me down but iss all right, iss all right," he said to himself and made a hissing sound between his teeth.

We sat quietly together. It was comic really. Kingdom was not going to do anything and never was going to do anything. Why did I let myself think such a thing and get into such a state?

Quite suddenly Tiny jumped to his feet, seized me by the wrist, and looked at me from frighteningly close range.

"One ting. Jus one ting will you do fa me?"

"OK, sure. What do you want, Mr Kingdom?" I stammered out.

Tiny gave me a look of infinite sadness and said, "Will you look after me dog, sah?"

I sat at the back of the ward office and let all the sound and chatter ride over me. Nurses came and went. The phones kept ringing, always the same greeting, "Mary Seacole Ward, staff nurse, can I help you?" They seemed very young. They kidded around a lot. Two kept flicking little balls of rolled-up paper at each other. I looked down at the pink section papers for Tiny and filled in the patient's full name and the ward name for *Place of Detention*. Then I ticked the box that said *Treatment Order Six Months*.

The voices drifted over me, "I can't remember jokes."

"How about this one? 'Good afternoon. Incontinence hotline. Can you hold please?'"

"That's pathetic, Sonia." Sounds of giggling. I felt too tired to be relieved. The world had simply taken another unexpected twist but the fear still lurked. I signed my name under the space for *authorising officer* and handed the papers to the charge nurse.

I picked up Kingdom's dog a few days later just as I had promised. Tiny's sullen parents handed it over to me. A stocky Staffordshire bull terrier. It was called Tyson. Brindle and white with pink mottled patches on its blunt muzzle. It had cabriole legs, a thick chest and triangular little eyes. I led it out with its studded collar and thick leash. Its claws skittered powerfully as it pulled along. I didn't much like dogs but felt an odd pleasure at its cocky truculence. I took it to a rescue centre for Staffies, I had no intention of looking after it myself. As I drove, the dog sat by me on the passenger seat, straining to look out. Its squat head kept moving obstinately from side to side, searching out the way.

# The Terror

The best of them were willing to learn from us but the worse were full of an unshakeable confidence in their own abilities. We surveyed them with a seasoned professional gaze, those new doctors coming to us for a six month rotation. Little did the young trainees know that the city swarmed with all manner of madness not dreamed of in their textbooks. Some, like Doctor Regan, even got to feel the terror just like their patients.

Regan was a little older than the others. She was a Registrar. An Irish psychiatrist in training. She looked like a flame-haired Rossetti heroine, a shapely Lilith with pale skin and cold green eyes. She had trained at the Irish high secure mental hospital at Dundrum. It must have seemed a high-walled and safe place compared to our porous city streets. She saw herself as medical aristocracy. Many of the maximum security forensic staff thought they had superior skills to us but we community workers knew that forensic patients had usually gone and done everything they were going to do. Community mental health was far more demanding and risky for we dealt in the unknown potentialities of our customers.

Regan glided into the patient reviews with her straight back and arrogant head. A trail of Hermès perfume followed her. Her long elegant nails tapped impatiently on the compact piles of case notes as she dominated the clinical discussions. She crossed and uncrossed her legs a great deal and the male nurses positioned themselves to get a better view. I also found myself drawn to her elegant and untouchable presence and enjoyed listening to the jaunty cadence of her brogue as she developed her authoritative views. Simon, the case-hardened lead nurse, noticed that I had been hanging around the new doctor.

"Out of your league, mate," he had growled to me in friendly warning.

Still, I arranged it so that I accompanied her on her first community assessment.

Her lovely green eyes surveyed me with repulsion, and a fine furrow of distaste appeared on her smooth brow as I explained how we operated.

"You mean, you see the patients outside of the clinics?"

I affirmed that we did. It was important to see them in their own homes.

"Well, we don't do that in Ireland." She was horrified at our demotic style.

So we met under the shadow of the tower blocks in a part of the city we called 'the mad mile', as the council had placed so many mental health cases there. The buildings loomed like giant domino counters. Bearded men in long robes were going to mosque while their women toiled back the other way carrying bulging shopping bags from the discount shops. Other occupants stood about in hooded coats as their bull terriers snuffled at empty chip packets.

We sat in my car looking through the referral notes. Her perfume filled the car. She looked a little perturbed that day. There seemed to be a faltering in that cool poise.

"Der's one ting I'd want to mention. I have a slight problem," she said. A vein pulsed ever so slightly at her delicate temple."It's silly really. I have a fear of animals. I'm frightened of dogs but in fact any animals — especially birds." Her eyes followed a flight of pigeons suddenly arrowing up past the blind windows of the blocks. Her lips were pressed tight. She must have been furious at having to reveal her secrets to me.

Her confession gave me a warm glow. I played the reassuring veteran as I led her through the pee-smelling corridors into the blocks.

The case was Mr Petridis, a Cypriot man in a vest who lived on the fourth floor. His dyed hair was trained up into a fuzzy rampart around his bald head. I asked him at the threshold of his flat if he had a dog.

"No, no dog," he answered. I glanced back at Regan to signify that it was safe to enter.

Mr Petridis had a fungal finger nail. It was all whorled and powdery like a piece of old cheese. He believed it was poisoning him, and that crumbly nail was a sort of portal that let evil things into his body. Doctor Regan seized command of the interview and began to question the patient. I sat back and gazed around his gloomy sitting room. There was a mismatched chess set with big red and white figures, some with the heads missing; a pyramid of used tea bags piled in an ash tray by his greasy armchair. On a stand stood a cheap porcelain figure of an owl with a card propped against it bearing the legend *I Lost My Heart To Cyprus*. In the deeper recesses of the room I could make out an object covered in a tartan blanket. I looked again. It was a brass stand with a scattering of chaff underneath. Not chaff but some sort of seed. Lord, it was a large bird cage.

Regan had focussed on Mr Petridis. She was intent on ferreting out all his delusions. I made a gesture to interrupt but she gave me a furious glance.

"Does your fingernail actually speak to you?" she continued determinedly.

"Well, no." The patient looked at his knobbly finger dubiously, "I do believe it is sending poison throughout all my body though."

There was a noise somewhere else in the flat. A clatter and a shuffling sound.

"Anyone else here, Mr Petridis?" I interrupted more forcefully.

Regan looked really annoyed at me.

"No, only Pumpkin," he said.

"Pumpkin?... Your wife, your partner?"

"Oh, no!" he laughed. "Pumpkin!" he called in a cracked falsetto.

A rustling shadow, a flicker, then down the corridor it came.

"Pumpkin!" Again Mr Petridis cried.

A large white bird flew straight into the room. It flared its wings in surprise at the visitors then flapped around our heads. There was a high scream from the doc and she lashed wildly with her notepad and referral forms in a vain effort to keep it at bay. This seemed to attract the creature. With a lunging motion, accompanied by a guttural squawking, it came down onto her head.

The bird seemed to get a firm grip and remained flapping and screeching, tightly clamped onto her red tresses. Regan leaped right up onto a sofa, her high heels wobbling. She kept batting at the bird with her papers. I rose and tried to support her by holding her at the hips. The bird continued to screech and cling to her hair. The owner reeled about in his vest, making grabbing motions, his armpits like black hairy holes. I tried to get her to lean over so I could get a purchase on her assailant.

"Just get it off me!" she was shouting.

I began to prize its rubbery grey claws from her hair while it flapped and emitted rasping screeches.

"You could have told us about the parrot, Mr Petridis," I said over the racket.

"It's a cockatoo," he replied as we both pulled at the shreds of Dr Regan's coiffure and avoided the lunges from Pumpkin's black hooked beak.

Doctor Regan alternated between screaming and whimpering until we detached the bird and confined it in its cage where it continued to squawk triumphantly. I helped her off the couch and we made our way across the feather-littered sitting room.

"I must get out of here," she wheezed as we hobbled along. She seemed to be hyperventilating, and I had to ask Mr Petridis for a paper bag into which I encouraged her to breathe until the panting subsided.

Afterwards we sat in my car. The flats rose barren and implacable above us.

"You will say nothing about this," she said as her composure returned.

Ever afterwards throughout the rest of her placement she exuded pure hatred towards me. She had been lost for a moment in a haunted wood and I had been a witness. The terror had opened up to her just like it had to her patients.

Months later, I was at my desk in our echoing old office building when I overheard Doctor Regan asking the nurses in their neighbouring office if they had any of the blank forms used by the doctors to authorise changes in medication.

"Haven't you got enough of these in your own office, doctor? You should always keep a few with you." It was Simon the charge nurse's gravelly unmistakeable voice. "After all, you know what they say, doc?"

"No? What is dat?" Regan replied in her tripping brogue.

"A bird on the head, I mean in the hand, is worth two in the bush!" said Simon. There was a sound of explosive sniggering from the nursing offices.

# Transference

Anyone could have recognised at the outset that she was a heart-sink patient, an abuse case, whom no male therapist should go near, but I blundered on with her for a whole year. Each weekly session became like an additional stone piled upon my back. It was not just her implacable grief that so afflicted me but also the growing sense that she had passed something on to me which I could never shake off.

I had accepted the case at our allocations meetings only because of pressure from my supervisor, who felt that I had not been pulling my weight. I had been seeing psychotherapy patients for a while. At first I had enjoyed the authoritative aspects of the role and the catharsis of deftly sorting out all those emotions. It had been a privilege to enter the lives of others and I felt that I was actually helping people. I knew this because they thanked me. Patients even sent me little cards telling me how well they were doing months after the sessions had ended. After a while though I began to feel a creeping burden that grew heavier the more patients I saw. Now, looking back, I can see that I was already beginning to drown. I drank at night to quell the squirming unease at the thought of another working day. I delayed my arrival at the office and sat smoking in my car, watching the stray cats climb across the old asylum walls at the back of the psychotherapy unit. There was a mirror right by the door to my consultation room. I began to get into the habit of staring into that glass for longer and longer. *Who are you?* The mask-like face gave back no answer. Sometimes I'd place my fingers on the reflection, touching that mouth, those accusing eyes. Perhaps I was trying to trace a response to my question. Well, in a strange way Brenda gave me that answer, but it was not the one I expected.

She had been referred by adult mental health services, a middle-aged woman with recurrent hospital admissions due to depression. She had been through the mental health system with no real clue to the sources of her distress, although childhood trauma could be guessed at. She had been patched up and sent along to the day hospital but had not really engaged with therapy there. She was eventually sent home with the latest antidepressants, back to the bungalow which she shared with her well-meaning husband. One day she took twenty Coproxamol tablets with her morning coffee after straightening the beds. She also took a handful of the antidepressants that had failed to change her hormone levels enough for her to feel better. She walked groggily to the field at the back of her garden, took out a kitchen knife with a serrated edge and, rolling up her sleeve, cut deeply at the dorsal aspect of her left arm down to the bone, severing the muscles, then she slashed round the other side to the inner arm, severing the ligaments but just stopping at the radial artery before she fainted at the pain. She was found by two frightened dog walkers. She had lost a lot of blood but survived and managed to avoid liver damage from the overdose. More treatment and hospital admissions followed. It became obvious that conventional answers to Brenda's problems were not adequate. Something different should be tried other than the blunt instruments of acute psychiatry. So I found her one February morning, reluctantly waiting for me in the psychotherapy waiting room.

She was a stout, homely-looking woman with indistinct squashy features and long, silky hair. On her left arm there was still a livid, purple weal and she kept it supported by a brace. She sat with her head slightly bowed, holding her handbag on her knees. It took months before she would lower that bag to rest it beside her. She kept her head down and murmured in a low, barely distinguishable voice. I was surprised that she kept coming to those early sessions. She was angry that I did not lead her to any topic or guide her. I simply opened the sessions and waited for her to tell me why she was there. I sensed the fury in her tense, bowed posture and by the speed of her departure as she hurried past me at the close. I also sat nursing my own wounds yet very aware of her smouldering, agonised, presence. The outside world would signal to us, the calls of children playing, the sounds of distant sirens. Silence would bloom between us; we would sit parallel to each other facing the clock. Sometimes she would tell me of her day, humdrum tasks she had performed, what her husband required for his tea, how she kept her home, what presents she had bought for her nieces. At other times she wondered aloud what to say to me and would speculate on what I wanted from her. She rarely asked anything directly but when she did her eyes would glare at me from dark, ringed pits while her face rippled with suppressed anger and pain. I endured her hostility and some days we said nothing at all the whole session. Little by little, however, over the weeks and months, she gradually began to tell me her story.

Once, she had lived as a plump and relatively happy schoolgirl with her parents in a southern suburb. Her father had been beaten, starved and brutalised as a prisoner of the Japanese during the last war. He had caught beriberi which had attacked his eyesight as well as weakening his legs. He spent his days in bitter rumination of the past, occasionally having a drink at the British Legion with the other ex-servicemen and spending time at a day centre for the blind. Brenda's mother had been stricken with breast cancer when she was still quite young. The disease had spread swiftly, bloating and distorting her body and killing her painfully. Brenda was taken to see her as she lay dying in hospital. She took Brenda's hand and whispered,

"You will be a good girl and look after daddy, won't you, dear?"

"Yes, Mam," promised the frightened ten-year-old Brenda.

Brenda tried her best after the funeral, helping her father in the house and working with an aunt who came in to do meals. It had been decided that father and daughter should stay together; there was nowhere else for her to go. She used to check his appearance before he went out, combing his hair and adjusting his tie, brushing scurf from his blazer with its regimental badge on the front pocket. In the evenings she would watch him feeling for his food, his fingers rustling over the table.

Sometimes she would hear him at night, calling out from savage dreams of the past. Neighbours also helped a little at home while she was at school and her maternal uncle arrived to lend a hand. All Brenda would say about him was that he was dark, short and bearded. She was not able to utter his name and I never actually found out who he was and thus he remained nameless. He was just called 'Uncle' in our sessions — elemental, evil, 'Uncle'.

Uncle had started to call in that first year, helping by driving Brenda and her father to the shops or to the Legion. He seemed at first to be a cheerful, helpful presence. He was a shift worker at a sheet metal factory and drove a smart dove-grey car. One day Brenda saw him as she came out of school. He called to her from his car, said he was passing and would she like a lift home. She agreed to go with him though she had not really known him well before her mother had died. He dropped her off, all the while promising her rides and little treats. Again in the following week he was waiting there for her. Soon he was driving her home at the close of every school day.

Whenever he was changing gear he would let fall his hand on her knee, or her thigh. At first it seemed accidental; then he left his hand there for longer periods. She felt uncomfortable but was too timid to say anything. Then swiftly, inexorably, his handling of her became more blatant and he began to pin her against the car or the garage wall with one hand while the other hand would rummage under her dress. This happened when her father was away at the day centre, and 'Uncle' would threaten that she would be blamed and put in a home if she told anyone and her father would have no one to care for him. Then he began to make her handle him while he briskly instructed Brenda in whatever gave him pleasure.

A routine began to develop every school day in the half hour before Auntie arrived to cook tea, Brenda would be pressed on her back onto the warm bonnet of the car. Sometimes he would even molest her in the house while her father fumbled about their living room or listened to the radio, complaining about Japanese products being advertised. 'Uncle' would silently thrust his work-roughened hands up her dress while also making cut-throat gestures in case she dared make a sound of protest.

The worst was when he used to force her to go to the upstairs bathroom of her house and run a bath. Then he would bathe her, washing his stain off her; his dark, hairy hands passing over her as she lay in the shallow water. She was terrified of him and prayed for the delivery of the school holidays when she could escape his presence to a degree. She feared that her father would be left alone if she said anything about the abuse and she kept remembering her promise to her mother to look after her father, so she endured it all without a word.

Brenda wrung out her story to me bit by bit in our weekly sessions and often I felt a sense of dread as I waited for her to arrive. In a way, I resented having to accept the heavy stone of her pain, and each session was an effort in endurance. At night, long after our sessions, I would listen to the therapy tapes over and over and then run scalding hot baths to try and wash her horrible story off me. I could not get her out of my head and began to stoke up a rage against the uncle. There was comfort in that. I started to develop strange violent fantasies. I used to think all the time about how it would feel if I could travel back in time to the 1960s to rescue her and to hurt him. I also began to plan how I might find him wherever he was now. I enjoyed thinking how I'd root him out and batter him, all tremulous and aged in some rest home.

Guilty thoughts about those others in my life whom I had not protected properly also bothered me. Sometimes child Brenda and thoughts of all the women that I had hurt would become blurred and intermingled and I saw them all as forsaken children lost in a dark wood.

My psychotherapy supervisor said that all this was negative transference. The supervisor was a Lacanian. She believed that the ego was unstable and urged me not to believe in the self that Brenda was projecting in the room. She termed it "the falsifying ego" and told me that my patient was factitiously superimposing upon me the role of both incompetent father as well as evil abuser, all rolled into one persecutory object. She urged me to work with the transference and to explore Brenda's feelings about me as a representative of her abuser. But the trouble was — being a poor parent and an abusive male was exactly what I was. Brenda was not projecting or falsifying. She had somehow found my essence. *Who was I?* I was both a bad therapist and a voyeur who had entered therapy for the worst of motives — for the vicarious pleasure of scuffling about in other people's inner lives.

It took months for Brenda to tell me what happened to her own abuser in the end. 'Uncle' continued to prey upon her until the time, at the age of fifteen, that she had met the man whom she was later to marry. It was a conventional, teenage romance yet it gave her resolve and she found the courage to fight Uncle off after five years, refusing him when he tried to touch her although he blustered and threatened, yet somehow he recognised that his day was done. He left her alone after that and she saw him just once more a year later on a family occasion which she could not avoid. They had stared at each other silently across the crowded room. Shortly after this she told me that she had heard he had been killed in a traffic accident. He just went off the road one night, and was buried without much fuss on the hilltop cemetery within sight of the estate where she continued to live. She went on caring for her father until his death and she managed somehow to forget those experiences, entombed in a safe but monotonous marriage. The memories had only come leaching back to torment her years later in the form of a depressive illness.

How disappointed I was! To think that this hateful man had escaped vengeance in a banal traffic accident. I even had the thought when she told me he was dead that I would dig him up, scatter his remains and kick his homunculus head around. I hid my disappointment from Brenda. She herself had survived 'Uncle' and she had survived the psychodrama of me as her therapist. Did she feel better for my help? And if so, what was the mechanism? Well, in a way she had outed me and that must have given her a pleasurable power. During those last sessions with her I used to think as she brushed past me into the therapy rooms that she was sniffing and scenting at me. It was only later that I realised that she was checking to see if I had successfully morphed in some way into a version of 'Uncle' and her blind father.

It was midwinter, the whole world frozen and therapy coming to an end. We had one last grinding session. She kept up an attack on me right to the end. Dissolution of transference had not taken place as it should have done according to the textbooks. My supervisor was concerned, but had little to go on as I had stopped telling her what was really happening. She had tried to tell me that therapy would be successful when the ego strength of Brenda became powerful enough to recognise that I, the therapist, was not one and the same as her abuser, and thus the transference would be dissolved. I had however realised that the transference in this case was much stronger than that usually allowed for by the prescribed doctrines of psychotherapy.

After the last session, Brenda turned to me in the corridor outside the therapy rooms and gravely expressed her gratitude. I, who had ministered conscientiously to her like a priest without faith, thanked her in return. I fancied that there was a twinkle of humour for the first time in her blurry face when we said goodbye and I noticed with surprise what a pretty, violet colour her eyes were as we came near to each other and we touched our hands together very lightly. She thanked me for listening and I wished her well but I also silently blessed her for releasing me. Once she had gone, I returned to my room and looked at myself in the mirror. I realised then that Brenda was better and stronger for our year of therapy and also that she, in turn, had helped me to see more clearly.

I thought about Brenda often in the years that followed but it took a long time for me to work out what had really happened in that room. I eventually realised that Brenda must have somehow understood through our sessions that language itself was not to be trusted. It had let her down. My therapy had been a failure of the word to convey the depth of her pain. She had perhaps believed that it would relieve her distress to express her awful secret story. She had also maybe hoped in some way that I, as a therapist, would have the knowledge she needed to absolve her from the abusive past. When it became clear that I obviously didn't have that knowledge and that words in themselves could not free her, my failure became her release. She grew into being her own expert by realising she did not need me and could treat me with contempt. She could be separate and strong, and that realisation was healing. Brenda had rejected the symbolic and learned to live with and accept her scarred but defiant self. I had also started to stir in the ashes. In that sense the bitter poison of Brenda's pain became a healing draught. Slowly, very slowly I began to feel my own dark wings moving at my back.

Brenda was my last psychotherapy patient. No more seeking my own answers through the wounded lives of others in those stifling consulting rooms. So, thanks, Brenda, wherever you are. You re-introduced me to that stranger — a dark angel who had really lived with me all my life: uncompromising, wilful and brutal, loving and hating equally.

# The Killing

I got used to reading homicide inquiry reports. I must have gone through hundreds of them in my time. It was my job to review the old cases to gain fresh insight on risk management. The attention got jolted though when the enquiry report involved you personally.

It happened in the last years of my career. I was called to be a witness in what was then called in the anodyne hospital phraseology, "a serious untoward incident review." That's putting it mildly. It was pretty damn serious and untoward. My patient had gone and killed someone.

You could see that Frankie was likely to do something nasty. I don't think we ever had any illusions about that.

It was just hard to work out how it could have been stopped. The inquiry examiners were looking for someone to blame. The investigation was run by a group of experts. I knew most of them. It was a year after the killing. The witnesses had been summoned to the hospital trust administrative centre. We milled around in silence in an ante-room. It was a sour anxious wait. We always dreaded that sort of thing, and the public inquests, which were even worse.

"Your documentation is very good. How effective were the plans in practice?" asked the chair of the panel when it came to my turn. In practice? I had many thoughts about what working with Frankie was really like. Memories of him were what you most wanted to forget but they kept shouldering in.

Frankie was wrong from the start. I remembered a row of shattered windows in the head injury centre where we'd first gone to see him. He'd trashed the whole of one floor. He was a nightmare and they were desperate to get rid of him. I recalled the bitter reek of smoke curling up from a ward toilet basin. There was a clump of burned plastic in there and a tangle of black-ened wires. Frankie had set fire to a transistor radio belonging to another patient. He didn't like the guy's music, in fact he didn't like any music full stop. He'd burn the patient next, he told us. Later, after he had been let out of hospital, I'd watch his broken silhouette moving under the street lights. I used to just sit and keep tabs on him from my car sometimes. He'd go stumping back from the pub, stopping to rain curses at any black people in his path. Even his poor old mother had become frightened of him after he had head-butted her front door.

"We can't have Frankie at home no more," she had said softly.

I'd also seen him on fire outside his house. He had set himself alight. Well, he was smouldering really. He had squirted an accelerant onto his clothing but the flames hadn't really taken hold. Something or other had upset him. He'd been doused down with foam and given a lesson about fire safety by the fire brigade. So, to answer the question, yeah, the plans had worked in practice right up to the time he killed someone.

Frankie had a sort of broken face. It looked like it had been glued back hastily together. It was a crude rubbery mask. All white and flabby and with little eyes that darted about like fruit flies. I had this rule with him, "Don't get in grabbing distance." I warned the other staff to abide by it. He could threaten and bluster but he moved his chunky body so stiffly due to his injuries that even the slowest could get away from him. The local children often scampered after him in the street and yelled "spazzo" at him. He'd turn and snarl but could never get at them because they stayed out of range. I'd read about red deer stags somewhere that when they meant to hurt you they just sidled up close making out they were doing nothing special, then when they were really near they would impale you with a sudden jerk. I guess the same was true for Frankie. You were OK as long as you remained out of grabbing distance.

He tended to be alright with me. I was straight with him and made no effort to be ingratiating. I just marvelled at how little he could exist on: no love, no friends, no books, no TV, no music, no radio, no ideas. Motorcycles were his only thing, even though they had nearly done for him. The sole decoration in his mean little rooms was a poster of a motorcycle racing ace.

What I knew of him could be rendered in long or short form. The actual inquiry report went on for eighty pages.

It was sufficient to know he'd probably always been a psychopath and was just made worse by everything that happened after. His father had left the family when he was three and was supplanted by a bullying stepfather. Frankie was slow in all his childhood stages. He had night terrors and explosive tantrums. He was in constant trouble at school. He was always punching the other kids and one account had him interfering with teachers' car tyres. In the end he was transferred to a special school for the slow and the delinquent. He left at sixteen and drifted through a range of jobs: bricklaying, roofing, door-to-door selling.

He somehow got his claws into an older woman with two children and the couple married despite his bad temper and his boozing. At the age of twenty-two he was found in a ditch having come off his motorbike. He had received a smash to the head and woke from two days of unconsciousness even more angry and disinhibited than he was before. The docs called it frontal lobe syndrome. That was shorthand for a blunted individual who had a poor attention span and savage tempests of rage. Frankie's wife and children became even more terrified of him. He heard voices telling him to do bad things. He tried hanging himself with a belt. He battered his head against walls or jumped out of windows if people did not agree with him immediately on any matter. He crammed down ketamine, speed, mushrooms, all sorts.

If that wasn't enough a few years later he slid his bike into a lamp-post and stoved in his head yet again. Maybe he was trying to rid himself of the world but he succeeded only in giving himself even more grievous damage. His occipital lobe had to be ventilated. He was re-sussed and a trache tube stuck in his neck. He was in a coma for a fortnight, then woke to raging aggression. His fuse was now even shorter. He was prone to pathological laughing or crying for no apparent reason. The cerebrospinal fluid could not vent out of his skull due to the head injuries and so his head visibly swelled up. The other patients called him 'Herman Munster'.

This is when we first saw him, rampaging in a head injury unit, trashing windows, throwing food and spitting in the faces of the staff. He wasn't much better on our secure ward. He set fire to bins, fanning the flames with a hairdryer. He'd yell at staff that he'd like to batter them and do time for it. Things got particularly bad when his wife told him she was leaving him. He broke a dinner plate over one patient's head and shrieked that he was going to shag and kill all the females.

The hospital ground on with him. They loaded him with sedation and sent him off on activities to soak off his aggression. One occupational therapist even took him horse riding. A brave soul, she was. Those poor horses, we joked in the staff room. The neurologists said that there would be no further improvement, but he gradually slowed down over the months. The manic energy was overtaken by the consequences of his injuries. He'd never been bright but now his intellect was so dulled that it hovered around IQ75 — the cusp of learning disability, although he retained an animal cunning.

Frankie had right side weakness. His hands flickered with palsy. He could hardly see properly and kept having epileptic fits. The inexperienced might have thought that he was too impaired to be truly dangerous, but he kept us on our toes. We found that he had levered a wooden shard off his door-frame to make into a shiv to stab a Pakistani patient that he particularly hated. A day patient had asked him to look after his pet dog for the afternoon. Frankie had told staff that he was going to take it for a walk in the grounds. They felt relaxed enough not to escort him. Straight off, he had made his way to the local vets and arranged for the animal to be put down. How he laughed at the dog owner's distress. Despite his potentialities there was talk of returning him to the community. His mother pleaded with us that he was not normal and should be put into an institution for his and everybody's sake. I agreed with her but the prevailing orthodoxy had ruled that Frankie could not be detained. The logic went like this: Frankie had a personality disorder. The law insisted that he could only be sectioned if he was treatable. No treatments had really worked on him. Ergo, Frankie was going to be let out to roam.

He ended up in Manwell Gardens next to the inner city allotments. The Gardens were a squalid grid of shanty-like timber bungalows built by the city during a housing crisis half a century before. They were probably meant to be temporary structures originally but they had proved useful as a dumping ground for the old, the disabled and the problematic, and so they remained. It seemed hard to believe that ordinary people actually lived there. The small wooden cabins with their tar paper roofs and warped guttering looked like a run-down holiday park for people of restricted growth. Fifty or so little shacks connected by narrow paths lined with heavy hedges of untrimmed privet. Frankie would totter along those alleyways all lined with dog turds, empty gin bottles and clumps of seeding goldenrod. He'd yell at his timid neighbours. Those poor grey wraiths took to hiding whenever he was on the move. Sometimes he'd spitefully stamp on their garden collections of gnomes, fairy mushrooms and plaster owls.

It was hard to keep an eye on him in that shabby warren. I used to park up on the main road that bounded the place and I'd only spot his squat lurching shape when he broke cover to go to the pub or to the Murco garage for fags. Despite my vigilance the obscure laws of life were already working towards him encountering his victim.

I had been particularly uneasy about him living in that collection of wooden buildings with his history of fire-setting, however he survived for a year or so there without any major incidents. I was relieved to hand the case over to a new worker as I was moving to another job in the ceaseless career mill of the hospital. I coached the new man in everything I knew about Frankie and reiterated my warning not to get in grabbing distance. Little did we know that Frankie was already in the trouble zone. I found out about it all later. How he had battened on to a seventy-six year old woman with one leg. Frankie wasn't choosy. She was called Mrs Santelli, a widow and a grandmother. She lived in one of the bungalows across from him. The family were apparently fairground entertainers and travelling folk. Somehow Frankie had been accepted by the old lady and let into her bed.

The new supervising worker did his best to steer everything away from disaster once he had found out that Frankie was disporting himself at a pensioner's place and was even taking her grandchildren to the shops to get sweets. They tried to prove that Mrs Santelli had dementia and thus was unable to consent to the relationship, but events soon overtook the slow movements of the authorities to protect the public. The wild card was Tonio, her son. He was in his early thirties just like Frankie. He lived in his mother's front room, never worked and lived by sponging and stealing off her and other folks. Frankie told the police that Tonio had picked him up one night on his way back from the pub and that had led on to meeting the mother. Maybe Tonio thought that the bumbling, slur-voiced Frankie would be an easy touch. Perhaps also he had been pimping his mother out and he had reckoned that sticking them both together would somehow further his ends. He was a handsome character with long dark tendrils of hair trained over his forehead that hid deep-set calculating eyes. As well as being a drunk he was also a doper, always sledged out on spacecake. He took on a hip-hop style and called everyone "dude", that is apart from Frankie, whom he called 'mong', 'spazz nuts', 'shite-eating dipshit' and worse. He must have thought he could handle the disabled idiot. No-one warned him about what he was really confronting though.

Tonio was young, lithe and strong. He played his hip-hop contemptuously, thunderously loud. All the neighbouring shacks used to vibrate to the sound. He loved crooning out those crazy choruses. He liked to snap his fingers and jig about in front of his bewildered old ma and her freakish lover. The authorities received a few signs of trouble. Frankie rang his new worker and complained that Tonio had stamped on his hand and abused him. The local police heard from Mrs Santelli about a necklace that somebody had stolen. Locals had to be dispersed after a rumour had started that Frankie was a paedo. Then Frankie was taken to Casualty after he had been clipped by a car. He told the Senior Houseman that Tonio had told him to go out and lie in the road and kill himself and he had followed his instructions. They increased his meds and more officials came calling. Tonio must have felt satisfied that he had crushed Frankie. Little did he know that this had just been a phoney war.

We usually have the illusion of an event towards which all things move in these enquiry reports. We are so linear, thinking time goes from left to right. Really though it's all a continuum, like a whirlpool. Tonio and his mother spiralling in their gyre and Frankie also in his circle of hell.

I glimpsed Frankie for a moment later that year around the time of the enquiry. He was rotting in maximum security, and I spotted him shuffling past me on one of the corridors. He nodded to me,

"How do? Mr M.?" he called out hoarsely. He was smiling and looked as fat and replete as a baby. He was obviously pleased with himself and content to wait for the cycle to come round again when one day he'd be on the loose once more.

I haven't told you what happened. The details hardly matter. It was there ready to come to pass. It was the work of a moment for it all to come together. Music and that close shoe-box hutch of a place, that's what did it.

Rain began to fall heavily one October Sunday night. It tapped on the tar paper roof and wonky windows of Mrs Santelli's bungalow. Tonio had been drinking rumble-gut cider all night. Frankie came round despite having been ordered not to by his minders. Tonio ignored him at first, then turned the sound up deliberately loud. The timber walls shook to the titupping beat. Frankie emerged from Mrs Santelli's bedroom and complained about the noise. Tonio told him to haul his shit-stained arse somewhere else. Frankie retreated and lay in bed with Mrs Santelli. Her leg was leaning against the wall. They watched TV but couldn't hear anything properly. At some point Frankie got up went to the kitchen and took out some scissors with long sharp blades. He hid them under Mrs Santelli's mattress. Hours passed, the autumn rain kept coming and Tonio went right on drinking and letting his sound system rip. Frankie re-emerged in the early hours. Tonio must have vaguely registered that doughy formless face.

"Oh, it's you, spaz man," he'd said. He'd let Frankie get really close. He just stood swaying about mockingly toasting him with a cider bottle. Frankie caught him with one hand and with the other he rammed the scissors up to the handles in Tonio's upper abdomen. Tonio didn't scream or anything. He just looked surprised, tried to get his mobile phone out to summon help then slowly collapsed onto the sofa. The scissor blades had nicked the pericardial sac and he was bleeding to death. Frankie pulled the wires out of the stereo then went back to bed. In the morning Mrs Santelli strapped her leg back on, went to make breakfast and found Tonio still on the sofa, the scissors sticking in him and the mobile in his hand. She called an ambulance. Yellow coats and smeared lights on a wet Monday morning. They manoeuvred awkwardly in the narrow pathways. Tonio was already stiffening. Mrs Santelli and Frankie were arguing violently in the bedroom. The scared ambulance men called the police. More uniforms arrived and all the inhabitants in the other bungalows stared out of their steamy little windows.

"The little shit deserved to die," was all that Frankie said to the cops. He seemed completely unconcerned.

The panel produced their report in the end. No staff member was judged particularly to blame. It was just the system that could not allow itself to lock him away. Frankie never wanted to be any different and nothing except time and the grim reaper were ever going to make him any better. The local paper had the headline *Why was he let out to kill?* Someone else took over his tenancy in cruddy Manwell Gardens. All those risk plans and reports went to archives and the families were left with their mountainous grief.

# The Stillness, the Dancing

Pat Haddon was a round, bustling woman whose pale eyes shone with desperate sincerity whatever lies came out of her mouth. If you saw her on the street, hurrying along, greeting her neighbours cheerfully, her Yorkshire terrier trotting after her, you would not guess the havoc going on inside. We had been asked to see her by a desperate housing agency. The rent had not been paid. There was a pest problem and large amounts of filth had piled up in her flat. I spent a winter visiting the place trying to persuade her to get help for her drinking and struggling to help her re-establish some order in her life. It was as cold as the moon in that filthy place and whenever I think of it I remember the bitter chill to my bones.

She was always desperately pleased to see me. Her relentless chatter filled the emptiness. I can now see that all those words were an attempt to stop me from doing anything to change her life. She did not really want to be helped. She just vaguely hoped that the bad things would be taken away so she could keep on drinking. I spent hours in that hideous place. She went over versions of her story again and again: telling me how love had gone bad, businesses had failed and how her family had been riven by pointless quarrels. To cap it all her husband had died and left her money, but she had run through it all. She lamented her fate and kept calling out for Poppy to comfort her. Poppy, her little bedraggled dog, seemed to do her best to avoid her erratic owner. She usually rushed away through the heaps of unopened mail, food containers, dirty clothes, tumbled furnishings, dead houseplants, stained upended mattresses and buckets of pee.

Strangely, there were never any empty bottles of drink lying about. She was oddly secretive like that.

I liked to think at the time that Pat had allowed me to see her genuine self only once, when I took her to a cemetery to pay her respects at her mother's grave. Her mother had died relatively young, one of the many disasters that had set Pat on her career of unhappiness. I sat in the car and waited for her while she attended the grave. And afterwards she sobbed deeply and long. I found out later that her mother had been cremated and the money I had given her for flowers had probably gone on Pat's own liquid consolations.

They evicted her in the end. Despite her endless prevarications and promises, she never did anything to help her situation. I contacted her daughter to see if she could offer any help. Her daughter told me she had previously tried to assist Pat by allowing her to stay in a caravan at the bottom of the garden but her mother's chaos had overflowed into her own house and she had asked her to leave in the end.

"You've met my mother," she said, "She'll not change. I'm trying to get on with my own life." Then she put the phone down on me.

So, Pat had to go to temporary accommodation. I was allowed back into the property for the last time to retrieve some items. Pat herself was too busy roaring complaints at the housing officials outside. I clambered over the filth to see if I could salvage something. I found a lamp, some once-fashionable grubby clothes which I stuffed into a bag and a reproduction Art Deco figure of a woman dancer. Then, in her reeking bedroom, I balanced on a pile of jumbled bedding to reach the top of the wardrobe and bring down her wedding album of long ago.

"Rather you than me, mate," said the supervising housing worker as a cloud of filth dropped down onto me as I rummaged.

I drove them both to the next stations of hell. Poor Poppy, that bundle of greasy fur, I deposited her at the dog rescue centre. I promised to get the creature back as soon as Pat had sorted herself out in stable accommodation. I then delivered Pat to a horrible place in the fag-end of the city, a Victorian house cut into flats for those on benefits. It was full of the emptyings from asylums and the broken shadows of men who had come loose from the usual structures of life. The ghastly dump echoed to the sound of sepulchral coughing and the thudding of hip-hop from the younger ones.

I completed the formalities with the skitter-eyed Asian owner.

"No violence," he said to Pat, pointing to a caved-in door of his office.

"Twat!" replied Pat.

"Is this all you can get me?" she hissed at me then she stomped off into a backyard lined with empty chip oil containers that served as plant pots.

"Our garden area," the proprietor had called it. There, Pat smoked fiercely and swigged at something in a paper bag. A few whiskery characters began to issue from the shadows and gather around her.

Pat's new room was in an annexe, a sort of Portakabin at the rear of the property. The only furnishings were a set of voluminous net curtains and a low bed. I set down her clothes, placed the Art Deco figure on the window sill and connected up her lamp. It was there that I first saw Michael, a quiet figure, the only other occupant of the shabby annexe. He held the door open for me as I entered with her possessions and he glanced over my shoulder at Pat who was loudly talking to the men in the yard.

"Your new neighbour," I announced.

"I see," he said in an educated voice, his grey eyes calmly surveying.

"He's been here for years," said the proprietor when I asked about Michael later. There was something genteel and courteous about him and I felt a curiosity. I often saw him on my return visits. I conjured up possible versions of his past. These places were filled with humble reformed sex offenders or woman-beaters but somehow it seemed unlikely that he was anything so vicious. There was something authentically ascetic and self-complete about him with his sparse frame and neatly trimmed beard. I wondered instead if maybe he was an alcoholic schoolteacher, a fugitive scholar or an ex-soldier escaping from some great disappointment. His room, when I glimpsed it, was always neatly kept. Once I managed to see that the book on his bed was titled *Great Essays in Science*. Michael himself remained elusive and uncommunicative.

That winter I came weekly, but Pat never did anything I asked her to do. She did not complete the application forms that I left nor make any attempts to help herself. She chattered on, leaping from subject to subject, telling me of reminiscences, vague hopes and plans, complaints or moans about the other male residents trying to get up her skirts.

Michael would let me in. I tried speaking to him but he always slid back into the shadows of his room. I asked Pat about him. Had he any visitors?

"No, thinks he's better than us," she said dismissively.

The only time I ever really got a hint of him was when I once found him gazing at Pat and her gang of reprobates in the outside yard. Someone had received a Giro benefit payment. All were in a gaggle, grabbing at the buff envelope and loudly speculating on the pleasures the money would bring.

"I hope you are not disturbed too much by them," I said, disloyally, about my client.

He replied, or I thought he said, "There is no feast without cruelty." He gave me a hint of a smile then he slipped back into his rooms. I wondered afterwards what he meant by that.

I came to those crummy lodgings one blowy March day bearing a housing application. Across the yard something was different. I knocked but there was no Michael to usher me inside. It was open anyway. My feet sounded on the hollow boards as I passed his room. His door was just open a crack. I rattled at Pat's door. There was a groaning inside as I entered.

"Morning, Pat."

Harsh light from a bare bulb, smell of staleness, stir-rings, Pat on the floor for some reason, covered in an old coat. Pieces of foil heaped with fag ends. Another shape pushed past me. I stood there in my jacket and tie, holding a briefcase.

"I'm not well, not well... he knows I'm not well!" Pat shrieked at the departing back of her nocturnal companion.

"Dirty bugger!" she added, but he was gone. "Any fags?"

I shook my head. I always gave the same answer but she still asked me every time. She got off the floor and sat on her bed scratching her head. She seemed to be fully dressed. I reminded her about the housing interview that morning. It had taken weeks to get it.

"I'm not good. I don't feel ready for it."

"If you don't go now then you will remain here another six months," I said wearily.

"Don't say that," she began to complain. "I don't want to know it. Them bastards want you to crawl. And you're not helping, always on at me."

I stepped out of her room. Sometimes the will to struggle with her was sapped. I used to have this fantasy when I worked in a long-stay asylum of what would happen if the staff just did not come to work one day. I spent hours thinking about the querulous faces of the inmates. Imagining what it would be like when they realised that they were at last truly on their own.

I stood in the dark hall on the thin matting. Something made me knock at Michael's door. There was no answer. I pushed it open. There was a strange dancing, dappled light around a core of stillness. Michael's net curtains were streaming in the open window, flickering over his neat little room. He was still in his pyjamas, half out of bed. His face was quite black. He had been dead for a while. Perhaps he had been getting out of bed, driven up by the nocturnal revelling of Pat and her cronies. A heart attack or stroke had probably killed him the previous night or maybe even the previous week. I looked down at him, held in utter silence, without thought, not ready for thought, just caught in the peaceful stillness of the dancing white curtains.

Then Pat came grumbling and banging about, "Where are you, Mr M.?"

"I'm doing something, Pat," I said, reaching for my phone but reluctant to break the spell. "You will have to wait just a while longer. We all will."

# The New Recruit

*For now we see as through a glass, darkly; but then face to face; now I know in part; but then shall I know fully, even as I am fully known.*
1 CORINTHIANS 13:12

I could just make him out in the sour underground light. It was winter. The diesel engine kept on clattering. I could taste the exhaust in the air. It came swirling in through the open door as the bus idled. Those sooty fragments went deep into the lungs. We had to accept our mortality and breathe it in. All dying a little bit each day anyway. That's when I spied him through the dusty window of the city express. He was leaning against a wall. A pair of large headphones spanned his woolly hat. He was holding a rucksack wrapped about with string and bungee clips. A complex web that only he could disentangle. He was still young for such a hard calling. Maybe thirty. It was hard to tell under all that dirt and beard scrub. His eyes were open but the gaze went inward. He made no evident sign of noticing the flow of people going past him in the busy station. He seemed to be concentrating on something though. He was scratching at his forehead in an absent-minded sort of way. These men lived in the mind and paid no heed to outward things. His jumper and hooded gilet were filthy. His soiled tracksuit bottoms were crammed into incongruous Wellington boots. I was pleased to see my stoic, shipwrecked accomplice.

I had been travelling to my job at the hospital. I enjoyed taking the bus although it was packed with citizenry. Like my fellow, maybe I wanted to be near to all those people yet not be touched by them. They somehow affirmed my singular, controlled world. There was a muffled clangour from the restless buses and the constant bubbling sound of voices. All those people seemed to be pouring on to a futurity that did not include me. I felt that my headphones man had the same melancholy preoccupations as I did. We both wanted to know how all those good folk endured their own unimportance, so disintegrated yet part of a larger ominous scheme of things. Like me, maybe my recruit was getting power from all their faces. His headphones had a trailing wire. He was evidently plugged in to the spirit of place. Both our worlds were as dense with significance as any psychotic's. I had a strange envy for him, as I did for all the hobos. I was snagged up in a job that I had begun to resent. I spent my days soaking up other people's sorrows yet my own starveling spirit yearned for escape.

The bus gave a start and the doors hissed. Soon we would jerk away and he would be lost to me for a while. I took a last look through the smeared window. He had straightened up and his bag was slung over his shoulder. He looked as if he was about to set forth on a journey. I had seen him a few times before. He had several stands in the city. My recruits usually had their regular beats. He could often be found outside a city centre chip shop all wreathed in the steamy exhalations of the place and ignoring the gibes of the clientele. Once I'd seen him in the hospital Casualty department. I had recognised those Wellington boots jutting out from under the plastic curtains of a treatment bay. I had been called to assess a young Bengali woman who had OD'd on analgesics and who'd had to be pumped out. She was murmuring her dismal tale of forced marriage, submission and despair while holding an infant and still occasionally vomiting bloody matter into a receptacle. I had tried to listen to her with sympathy yet my attention was on my man. I wondered what had brought him to Casualty, and I followed his progress through the triage area as the night went on. He gave no clue to what was ailing him. No one seemed to say anything to him. He sat on a gurney surveying the turbulent sorrowful scene with mild grey eyes and eventually he just slipped away.

\*\*\*

I called them 'recruits' but they seemed to choose me really. The first had been 'Father Christmas' or 'Fred' as he was also known by the locals. He was a whiskery cheerful vagrant glimpsed for years as I went about my community psychiatry visiting rounds. He gradually assumed significance for me. I found something comforting about seeing his raggedy figure and that yellowed knotted beard. If you went near him you could hear him singing dirge-like hymns to himself and he would call out, "God bless you," in an accented voice. He made me feel better. I felt that I was looking out for him and maybe he was for me in some strange way. Local Sikhs and Hindus brought him food. I think they thought of him as a holy man and a renunciate who had set aside life. And maybe that is what he was. I gave him money once. He looked at it with surprise in his brown leaf-like hand. He was still staring down at it as I walked away. He had set himself up in a niche in a church wall next to a busy road. He sheltered himself with a tarpaulin screen and at night you could see tea lights flickering around him like a shrine. Sometimes he would take a broom and sweep the roads around him.

Eventually he was found dead one winter in his niche. The newspapers said that he was possibly a Polish soldier who had worked for the Nazis in the war and had wanted to expiate his crimes. I didn't really believe it. It sounded like a secular myth put about to diminish his memory. He was so much more than that.

Then there was Chris. I had first known him twenty years before. He wasn't so obviously an outsider then. He used to drift around the city pubs, always sitting outside. I talked to him few times. He spoke awkwardly as if he had learned a new language with difficulty. Just a few pleasantries passed between us. He pronounced his words stiffly, the locutions all barbed and twisted. Sometimes he'd repeat a word to himself as if he found the sounds themselves curious. I found myself buying him a drink while my friends made faces. They had sensed that there was something odd about him. The only thing I remember him telling me was that he had once studied physics at university. Perhaps it was true. The trackless years passed; one merging with the next. I saw Chris occasionally. Street corner chats. He gradually morphed. His thick chestnut hair turned into blackened, felted dreads, his outdoor tan hardening to a pan of caked filth. His shy bear-like eyes remained the same though. He settled to a mendicant life. Sleeping under the rhododendrons in a public park and begging in the city. His speech and social skills deteriorated over the years but we kept up a connection and he seemed to remember me whenever I encountered him.

I only tried to help him once during one hard winter. I used to see him close to the hospital where I worked, a tall figure hobbling from his night roost in a cramping frost with just a ragged blanket over his bony shoulders. I arranged with a friendly Casualty sister to give him a hot drink each morning. More ambitiously, we plotted to clean him up and give him new clothes. One quiet morning we used the hospital facilities to bully him into taking a shower. We also snipped off some of his encrusted hair and trimmed his gritty beard. Chris was furious but acquiescent. I felt we had done a good thing as he loped out scowling into the chill air. My colleague reported that she saw him ripping and soiling his replacement clothes in the hospital car park. Maybe he thought that a successful beggar was never a clean one.

A few years remained. Chris took to wearing a plaster cast almost permanently on one leg — perhaps it was another begging ploy. I used to see him indomitably stumping along with a walking stick and dragging that duff leg. His hair had grown to form a great tangled nest. He looked like a beggar king with his wand of office as he took his alms from passersby. Whenever I saw his great black beetling shape enduring everything I also found my own hurts and trials felt somehow lighter. Then one day he just didn't seem to be around. After I hadn't seen him for a while I checked with my sources: a friend in medical records, the police, the coroner — nothing. Chris had just slipped away back to whence he came.

Raincoat Man gradually took his place over time. He could turn up anywhere, distinctive in an olive military mac and bush hat. He specialised in the ring roads that looped around the city. You would just glimpse him from the car window or in the rear view mirror. A limping, grimacing figure. He seemed to hobble along very slowly while his head and upper torso twisted about and he bared his teeth as if every step was bringing him terrible pain. In later years he used a stick, then two sticks, so I guess there was something actually wrong with his legs or feet. It was hard to see because of the long coat. His feet were usually clad in white trainers. Often the thick laces trailed behind him like old bandages. Whatever it was, he dragged himself along as if in mortal agony. There was something very disturbing about him. I often used to sit and watch him from my car. He would take an hour to cover a hundred yards. He reminded me of those pilgrims who climb to mountain shrines while whipping themselves or crawling on thorns. I'd see his hunched tormented shape miles out in unusual neighbourhoods dragging himself on through the vehicle spray and I'd wonder where he was going. What was he searching for? Sometimes I'd have the strange thought that he was somehow paying for all our sins. Raincoat Man, our scapegoat.

Once I spotted him in unusual territory, a run-down inner city area. He was being followed by a gang of kids who were hurling rubbish at him. I pulled up and shouted at the children. They ran off, shrieking abuse back at me. He was already limping slowly away. I approached and called out, "Are you alright, mate?" His raincoated back did not cease bobbing. I could distinguish a low moaning sound coming from him. His bush hat did not turn. I had to speed up and get around him before confronting him. I felt strangely anxious at interrupting his penitential progress. A pale, wet, narrow face under the shadow of the hat brim. Reddish stubble, sunken eyes that would not focus on me, auburn hair matted down to rat tails by drenching sweat. His open mouth showed teeth like yellow rocks. He gave a terrible groan and slowly crabbed past me. I persisted in trying to communicate. He gave a louder moan and raised an arm as if to ward me off. I felt sorrow at having so disturbed him. He shuffled away, *step, step, groan, step, step, groan.* Papers blew over the pavements around him. A flicker of rain came from a loaded sky. I felt awed and frightened by his implacable mysterious purpose.

Later, I made enquiries. One psychiatric team told me he sounded like a man they had once tried to help. They'd settled him into accommodation but they found that he kept tunnelling under the walls and endangering the building. Eventually they had to discharge him. Maybe that wasn't Raincoat Man at all. No-one was really sure. Vagrants and wanderers usually escaped psychiatry They didn't really count. To go mad you needed a settled place in life for the system to claim you. As for Raincoat Man, eventually I realised that five winters had passed and I had not seen him. Maybe he had finished his pilgrimage and found rest at last.

\*\*\*

My chap was still there. The driver looked at his watch, glanced up at the station clock then shut the bus doors with a hiss and a clunk. The diesel engine hammered and we began to roll. I took a last look at Headphones Man. I knew not when he would appear to me again. It would be a dry year if I did not see him.

He remained in shadow, unbidden and unexpected. His mouth was pursed from tasting all his grief — bitter and sharp with stalks. His blackened fingers carried auguries. All his kind were my muses. They waited out the hours or the interstices between the hours. They kept a watch for me and taught me that the secret of happiness was to stop caring so much for what I had not got and instead to accept all that I had already in my grasp.

The bus swung to exit the station. I twisted round in my seat, ignoring the fixed stares of my somnambulant fellow passengers. He was just to be made out. A dark blurred figure. He raised an arm. It seemed like a hieratic gesture, a signal to me. Headphones Man, greyhound of futurity! He had accepted his recruitment. His job was to remind me every time I saw him that I must do things while I had passion to enact them. He and all my recruits stood there at the imminent door. They were going on before me. Scrying out what was now hidden from me.

# One in Seven

"One in seven," said Doctor Ryan, marching crisply along the front row of the audience. He ventured further down the aisle of seated attendees, "One in seven of you," he indicated a group of us in a mock count off. His finger came to rest at the seventh, pointing at me. We gave a collective involuntary shudder; some chuckled and exchanged defensive glances with their neighbours. The mood was edgy. He had certainly got us going.

"Yes, research has indicated that one in seven in the population have a diagnosable personality disorder. That includes you." He hopped nimbly back onto the dais and clicked up a new display screen taken from the *Journal of Clinical Psychiatry*. It showed the ten personality disorder types and their relative frequency in the population. Obsessional 'PD' was streets ahead of the rest followed by 'emotionally unstable disorder'.

*Which one of them are you?* I thought sourly, *Narcissistic probably.*

Ryan was a new buck, a consultant in charge of the dangerous and severe personality disorder programme in the high security hospital. He was not much liked by those of us who worked in the general wards. We thought he just cherry picked the perverts and the more exotic cases. He was a young Irish doctor with a goatee and a green tweed jacket with shiny leather patches at the elbows. There was something about the Irish that was attracted to forensic. No end of their doctors on the secure wards.

Ryan was keen on the new therapies that promised to treat the untreatable: Dialectical Behaviour Therapy, Schema Therapy and Mentalisation. Their glossy new names ushering in new regimes. The old cure for dangerous PDs was time. Long shrouded years of institutional time. Most of us older clinicians thought we would keep a weather eye on these modish new cures. We would suspend judgement until they were tested out in the intractable coils of our stubborn patients. Ryan had arranged this conference with the Met to discuss predictive likelihood of serial homicide in professionals following the Shipman trial, the case of the murdering GP. Ryan had focussed on personality disorder as being the most evident risk vector. He further irritated us when he put up a Greek word, $\mathring{\eta}\theta o\varsigma$ on the screen. He looked at us challengingly. Study of the classics had eluded most of his audience. The policemen there looked particularly baffled.

"Ethos," he pronounced. "It means ethos. We usually think that ethos refers to the idea of a set of guiding beliefs or morals." The audience nodded. Ryan went on, "Ethos originally meant in the Greek 'the accustomed place'. It came gradually to mean the prevailing character and disposition of individuals which in turn influences the moral climate of the societies in which they live. In classic Greek drama the interplay of the actors with the audience created the desired ethos in the audience." Yes, OK, but we wondered where he was going with it. My neighbour, a grizzled psychotherapist, leaned over to me and whispered, "Know thyself, that's Ancient Greek as well isn't it? Well I know I'm bored stiff with this guff already." He emitted a wheezing laugh like an old gate hinge.

Ethos, the word continued to shimmer ominously on the screen.

*What was my 'accustomed place'?*

Not here certainly, a wolf in the fold. Ryan boomed on, "I say that instead of forcing our ethos on our personality disordered patients we should shape them from the inside. There are three categories of ethos in the traditional Greek plays. *Phronesis* — practical skills & wisdom, *Arete* — virtue or goodness, *Eunoia* — goodwill towards the audience. In our work in the hospital we are putting fresh life into these old categories." He began to list how the new therapeutic approaches promised to mould, reset and revalue the inner lives of the patients. The police looked discomfited. They had wanted some sort of forensic run-down that could predict dangerous professionals, not this classics shit. My gaze shifted to the nursing staff standing at the back. Bulky men with folded arms and buzz haircuts. Nurses were always more dangerous than doctors. Doctors had the compensations of status. Nurses were always chippy. Add a PD or Münchhausen's twist to that and you were cooking.

116

The wind blew all year long in that elemental place. Beyond the barred windows of the conference suite, clenched balls of muscular cumulus were driven along. Shreds of plastic jigged in the perimeter wire. Where did all those plastic bags come from? Probably lobbed out by the patients from the cell windows. Easier to shit in a bag and throw it than wait to go to the latrines. Ryan wound up at last with something about Greek drama and masks.

I think he was saying that ethos meant that dangerousness was contextual and that the patients could free themselves from the repetitions of their disorders by changing their relation to others. It was a long-winded way around it. The audience resented being dragged through a lecture. We split into groups to discuss the issue of the day. I kept feeling like there was something stuck deep in my throat. Something scaly or bony. No-one really wanted to discuss the set topic — dangerous professionals. The jolly medics gossiped about expenses and hospital politics and did not really engage. They had no intention of lifting up their own carpet and looking under it. Psychiatry was not a place where professional disclosure was encouraged. The gritty nurses likewise would remain clamped. The quarrelsome psychologists — now they would ferret after secrets. They might have been the only ones willing to debate the issue. I drifted around the chattering groups. I had an odd urge to confess and bear witness. What would I tell them? I kept having to clear my throat.

I knew well enough where I scored in the personality disorder scale. I'd done the screening tests on myself. Strange how so few of my colleagues risked that self-diagnosis. The types of disorder were as many as on the fingers of each hand. These in turn were grouped into three clusters, the odd or eccentric disorders, the dramatic disorders and the anxious ones. Where did I fit? Let me count the ways.

I hit high marks in two groupings including that toxic cluster two that housed the anti-social or psychopathic. I also had a good dab of schizoid in me — a chip of ice in the soul. Legion, that was my name. I thought it odd that my colleagues had not identified me as a PD. Reciprocal probably. Still I had a yen to shake them up a bit. Shock 'em. Like those times I went to substance abuse conferences and wanted to tell them about how wonderful it really felt — that first hit of crank going up your arm.

Everything I owed was to the PDs. They were my peeps. I was one and the same as them. They had rescued me from the tedium of dealing with the fuzzy stupor of the psychotics and the dreary whining depressives. They had helped me heal. They had recognised my scars and appreciated the way I had dived down deep with them. I had sucked the bitter smoke down to the lung root with them and came up the other side. Ryan was right in one thing. I admitted it grudgingly. The PDs were not static. They always had another side to them. Their duality gave them both their charm and their menace.

What could I tell these professionals at the conference? The blank-eyed senior registrars pegging their way grimly up the ladder. The consultants in their armour. The impressionable juniors so eager to please. The foreign staff earnestly taking down notes.

*Oh give me my real people!*

My PDs would have soon mixed it up in that arid conference. You know, there were some psychiatrists from the biological wing who actually claimed that severe PDs did not dream. They used it as a diagnostic indicator. Yet, we were soaked in dreams. Dreams enough to set fire to the waking world.

*They would be better off studying Shipman's prede-
cessor, the good doctor John Bodkin Adams, late of
Eastbourne. Now he was a killing doctor like no other and
never convicted. Look at the man in detail and you will
find the risk.*

I sometimes thought that the diagnostic scale of the
PDs reflected the seven deadly sins.

*A proud look. A greedy belly. Hands that shed innocent
blood. A heart that devises wicked plots. Feet that are
swift to run into mischief. A deceitful witness that uttereth
lies. Him that soweth discord among brethren.*

You would want them with you in a war though, and
in these moronic times give me a PD every time rather
than the average homogeneous, politically-correct citizen.

Like Brian Bolter. The doctors at the conference
would have tabbed him for an anti-social PD but even in
his savagery he had courtesy. He had fourteen convic-
tions for assaults. He used to come to the office, his pale
eyes holding me.

"Sorry to trouble you, Mr M. You see I've gone and hit a
man again." I used to just listen to his latest tale of
disaster. He usually had fights with security guards. He
didn't like their rude manner. In my heart I couldn't
condemn him. He once noticed when I gave him a lift somewhere that I carried a metal pipe under my own car seat for
protection on the streets. He nodded with approval. It was
the only time I saw a smile on his serious face. Still see him
on the street sometimes. He makes a point of coming up
and greeting me: "How are you keeping, sir?" A firm handshake and a torching stare. Somehow I'm glad he is
surviving his asperities, keeping to his code. I thought him
admirable according to his lights.

And Stuart Pearl, one of the most paranoid men I'd ever
encountered. Not deluded, it was just the set of his character. I was taking him once to a hospital appointment in

119

my Celica. It had taken ages to get him out of his house. He kept checking for enemies and threats. Standing in traffic, a big travel-stained delivery truck suddenly took into its head to go backwards. The reversing lights lit up. The engine gunned and it started reversing back onto us. We watched the great back of the thing like a looming cliff. I sounded the horn and engaged reverse but it kept on coming. We had been jammed up by another car behind. Stuart said not a word. Just watched the worst happening. There was a rending crunch, our vehicle bucked. The back of the truck rode up onto my bonnet. Steam erupted from shorn pipes. I got out thinking, "Shit. Stuart is going to go ape." All he said after climbing out the wreck with dignity was to ask after me, "Are you alright?" Perhaps dealing with his disorder was the hard thing. The dangerous real world was nothing compared to that.

They often had a courage to them and an acceptance of the nature of things. The PDs taught me a lot. They taught me the true moral of the story of the 'Beauty and the Beast'. That to be loveable one must be loved.

Paramvir Sood, now. He'd have plunged through that conference like a maddened steer on the loose. His name meant "supremely brave", he had told me. He was what they used to call a severe borderline or emotionally unstable PD. His wife actually had the mental illness. He was just so chaotic and demanding that they asked me to work with him so that his wife could be treated. He was an explosive man, always changing moods, shifting like a thundercloud. He would try and shower gifts on me or ply me with cups of sickly cardamom-scented tea and then as quickly he would be yelling and bashing his own head with his plump soft fists. Once, when I'd read a letter out that told him he wasn't going to get a council tax rebate, he bit his own arm then with a histrionic scream ran out his front door and started to clamber over the metal railings outside. He was on the second floor fifty feet up. The shoppers in the precinct below scattered at the sight of a fat Indian man in a vest about to splat down. I hauled him back over the rail by his hair in the end but he didn't resent me for it.

When I used to visit Mr Sood I'd often find him chanting in a fume of incense at a little shrine to the four-armed goddess Lakshmi in the corner of his front room. It was a small cleared space among all the debris he used to collect from building skips and bins ("Valuable items the English do not want, Sahib"). He'd be chanting, "Om Ganesh, Om Ganesh, dear Mahalakshmi, O let my lottery numbers come up!" Then he'd shake a small plastic tumbler device that selected tiny numbered lottery balls. He never got a win but he certainly came up good the day he saved me. After leaving him one day I got cornered by three youths outside in the piss-stained stairwell. They were keen to rob and mess me up. I read it on their mean scrawny faces that they meant business. I was backing up slowly and considering my options when there was a high-pitched shriek from behind. Sood came running down the steps, barefoot and wild-looking, with a coffee table raised high over his head. He hurled the table straight at my assailants. It splintered loudly on the concrete steps. The unnerved street scum promptly fled.

"Now, Sahib, you really must take better care with these fellows about," he said in between bouts of puffing and blowing. He was really chuffed to have rescued me. I thought of the burden of being indebted to him. But that was not to be. Poor old Soodie was felled by a heart attack not long after. I was invited to his funeral. There he was, garlanded in his coffin in his front room. They had cleared out all his clutter. Turbaned greybeards filled the place, chanting and waving joss sticks. We formed a ring and danced around his bier and scattered rose and

121

jasmine petals onto him. He gradually disappeared under a pink mound of them. In the end just his stubborn face still showed through.

*Those medics and mental health professionals relied too much on theory. You needed to live on the skin to really see what's coming.*

I finally got sick of the conference. I could have told the men from the Met that I thought a lot of the dangerous prisoners and patients deserved to be dead for what they had done. But it was not me who was risky, it was men who did not know what was in their hearts who did real harm. I went out through the hospital security gates. A thieving winter dusk was eating up the day and rooks waddled in the wet car parks.

*Let there be no more eschatologies for me. We should be like riverbed stones rubbed smooth by life. Element on element.*

Driving home from that numbskull conference, I kept thinking for some reason of Jack McBurnie. A small angry Glaswegian, a narcissistic PD exacerbated by drink. He could be very charming and I liked him for his strange honesty. I'd listen to his troubles and give him £10 from the work petty cash sometimes. No other staff would go near him. Tried to head butt me once but he was so short he bounced off my chest. He was very apologetic later, "I didnae mean it, sir," he said.

I didn't hold it against him. Turbulence came with the territory and there was a likeable roguishness about him. As I let him out the building he used to joke, "Och, Mr M. They broke the mould when they made me. Aye, one in a million, that's me." He would turn to shake my hand then spin round once more for his punch line, "And they beat hell out of the mould maker too!" Skirl of laughter as he drummed down the steps and out into the wide windy street.

# From a
# Distance

I see you from a distance sometimes. I recognise your uncompromising step. Always straight, like an arrow that has just left the bowstring. My gaze follows your bristling narrow shape along the suburban streets. You must be hurrying to or from work. I see you in every season. Unmistakeable, in a long tan raincoat in autumn, scarfed and gloved in winter, tweed jacket the rest of the year. There is something of a shop dummy look to you, a mannequin stiffness that plays against the springy tension of your stride. I do not need to be near to make out your waxy features, your neat cap of now greying hair, clipped moustache, deep pool-like eyes. That

Adam's apple like a fist. I observed you at close quarters for a year of group therapy so long ago. Now I watch and remember from a distance. I marvel and rejoice every time I see you that you are still there holding to your direct course. For you and I are fellow travellers. We follow the same path. Who have we to help us now that therapy is ended? Not people certainly, nothing supernatural neither, yet we both must withstand a terror that we can scarcely endure.

How did you get to that group psychotherapy a decade ago or longer? You had tried really hard to rid yourself of your physical form. You had checked in to one of those inexpensive new hotels with a minibar and no meddling room service. A summer dusk was falling on the city. You proceeded with single-minded efficiency to try and kill yourself thrice over. First, a handful of paracetamol chased with whisky. Next, you wrapped a noose of electrical cable around your neck and looped it over a radiator pipe. You then stood on a low stool and fitted your head into a plastic bag and even tried to seal it with gaffer tape. It got difficult after that. You were groggy from the tablets and the bag kept getting all steamed up but you went on with it. When all was secured you stepped off the low stool and that should have ended it. Then life threw in a wild card. Incredibly, a maintenance worker let himself into your room chasing a plumbing fault.

Revived, survived, you sat through my group with seven other suffering souls. You hated us that whole time. We never got to really understand why you tried to end your existence. I suspected a metaphysical despair rather than cruel love. Once you even sat silently in the session with a cardboard sign that you had fashioned into a sort of hat. It read, *this group is crap*. But you waited us out like a prisoner doing a sentence. You endured us

124

and we you but maybe we all found a new way of going on.

I watch you through the years from a distance. You and I obviously both know we are not reliably at home in our interpreted world. There remains for us only the comfort of yesterday's habit, the loyalty of familiar objects, the routine of that narrow path. Perhaps I should declare myself to you, my brother, my double and we could make our way together before it is too late? I only see you in the daylight. For both us it is the silent explosion of night that must bring terror when the wind, full of dizzying space, gnaws at our features. You have found a way to proceed by keeping to your prickly undeviating way. Go on my friend. Put some distance down. For both of us that old fairy tale holds true — which arrow flies forever? It is the arrow that has hit its mark.

# Brilliant

Only in retrospect do we bestow significance on fateful places. At the time they seem as banal as any other. One such was the view from my office window some years ago. It looked out onto a courtyard garden at the centre of the psychiatric hospital. A crook-stemmed Japanese acer grew there next to a bench. Its leaves were dull green all summer; they then blazed fiercely in the autumn before covering everything with fallen crimson. Katie took herself under the tree all through the winter. She usually did it on a Friday when nursing staff were distracted and there was a rush to clear work. I rarely saw her arrive. I had a job that was slowly grinding me down with the weight of responsibility. The phone rang all day long with urgent demands to be met and a stream of staff brought their anxious faces to my door for guidance. At some stage I would look up and she'd be there on the bench under the tree. The same dim slumped shape in the grey watery shadows of the little garden. She would usually slip out of her ward on the first floor and sneak down into the courtyard. She would often take a load of booze and pills all at the same time or she would gouge at her arms with a blade. Then she'd just remain out there in the cold. She had a knack of merging with the background, of being invisible in some way to the staff who hurried down the windowed corridors that spanned the little garden space. I had no idea why she hurt herself or staged her collapses like that. At the time, it seemed like just one more hassle in my overcrowded days.

Usually, after spotting her on the bench, I would leave it a while in the hope that someone else would deal with the problem. The light would begin to fail in the winter afternoon, still the stubborn shape would be there and if the ward had not come to fetch her I would leave my hot arid office and go out to see her. It was strange to confront her guttering there in the twilight. There would be the smell of wet leaves and of earth. Katie, sitting or sometimes slumped over or occasionally lying the full length of the wet bench. She often wore baggy lumberjack-type padded shirts, darkened with moisture like tide marks. She was only young. Maybe late twenties. It was hard to see her face; it was always cradled or hidden in her arms. Once I tried lifting her head to try and make out her features. But she retracted herself inwards as if pulling into a shell. All I could make out was a babyish, unformed cheek, silvered by tracks of mucus.

I didn't really know her. She was just one from the slow stream ward, the 'slow rehabs' which was the name the hospital gave to the no-hopers. Sometimes as I stared down at her, I allowed myself to speculate how all her hopes must have closed down to get to this place. Mainly though, I simply felt stressed at having to sort out yet another mess on top of my own job. When cajoling made no effect, I would attempt to tug her upright but she was heavy and her bulky arms in their blood-stained sleeves would fall slackly to her sides as I tried to wrestle with her. Usually I just ended up rolling her into the recovery position. I'd go back to my office and ring the ward and an irritable charge nurse and nursing auxiliary would come and drag her back upstairs. Occasionally a reluctant ambulance would be summoned if she had taken a particularly heavy load of pills.

Her appearances came to a peak then they dropped off. Maybe she was being watched much more carefully. Occasionally, I'd look up from my piled desk on a Friday that late winter and just see the empty bench under the bare tree and wonder briefly how she was doing. Then the surging pressures of work shunted her out of mind. I had other suffering faces to puzzle over.

Cruel spring came on. In the courtyard garden tulips nosed through. Big orange Darwin tulips. Then there was Katie back in her usual spot. I came out to find her lying on the bench as the fresh sun reached into the courtyard to light up the silky furious petals. She was lying with her face hidden as usual. I called to her and leaned down to look at her and this time I realised that she was not in a semi-conscious state but instead was looking deeply into those raging tulip blossoms from close range. She turned her head and looked straight at me for the first and only time. A pale blank face like the moon lasting into day. She pointed with one of her razor-scarred clumsy hands.

"Them flowers, brilliant," she whispered hoarsely.

"Yes, aren't they great, Katie."

I nodded and smiled to encourage her, thinking that

at last here was a muddled, blunted consciousness seeing the joy in nature. But that was not it at all.

I rotated to another post and was glad to leave the institution and the sense of suffocation from being close to all those poor devils choking out their lives on the long stay wards. Six months or so later I returned to the hospital on another job and bumped into Greg. He was a rehab nurse manager, bull-necked and gruff. Like most ward nurses he never seemed to speculate much on the inner lives of the patients. He was hunched in an alcove, smoking an illicit cigarette, not far from my old office window. I stopped to chat and we both watched building workers setting up a new security fence as the hospital continued to expand relentlessly.

"What's been happening?" I asked.

"Usual shit," said Greg. "We had a right hassle after you had gone. An untoward incident. That Katie. Big fat girl?"

Oh yes, poor old Katie.

"Well, she fooled us good. She cooked up a plan. Hid in a stairwell cupboard during shift change. Wrapped herself in toilet tissue. Round and round like a bloody mummy. Then sprinkled lighter fuel all over herself. Burned up before we got to her. We found her flailing around the garden all on fire." He grimaced and flicked his fag butt away. "Finito."

So Katie had joined the other souls that seemed to trail after me. We all knew that spring was the time for suicides. April and May saw twice many as any other time of year. Somehow the new light summoned them but Katie, keeper of the ancient flame, had gone one better. She had truly donned garments of fire.

# The Fire Game of Nil

If anyone was going to discover the meaning of life then it would have been Kris Krajewski. To me, he bore the signs of a full grade genius. He had told me that he was on a quest to find the source and template of the universe. He was not special to the medics though. They tended to view all his products as those of illness. Their aim was to return him to being a normally functioning person. According to them, his odd ideas were the fruits of delusion and needed tackling just like his synaesthesia had to be rubbed out. Yes, not only had he the bitter fortune of being diagnosed with paranoid schizophrenia, but he also experienced unusual neurological effects whereby visual and aural sensations fired up along the same nerve pathways. Kris's mind twirled in a kaleidoscope of interconnecting sensory patterns and this made doubly certain that the docs had made a judgement on him. Whenever I persisted in challenging orthodox views on Kris in clinical discussion I could tell that they viewed me as being well-meaning but misguided. I had a sneaking sympathy for psychotics anyway. I felt they often had an enviable seriousness of purpose. They were trying to establish new forms of order in a spongy world that shifted under their feet. It seemed ironic to me that conventional psychiatry worked so hard to destroy their delusional systems whereas it was just those constructs that so often kept them from dissolving entirely into truly deep madness. I thought that Kris's mental world went beyond the usual defensive psychotic schema. I saw him as a savant brimming with strange powers. Psychiatry, however, did not care for extraordinariness. They were bureaucrats of the brain, intent on making a straight way.

I persisted in questioning our pharmaceutical approach to Kris. I cornered Dr McPeake about it in a tea-break after our case allocations meeting. He was a youngish ambitious psychiatrist in charge of Kris's care. His speciality was quantitative rating measures for depression.

"Look, you need to understand," he said putting down his doughnut, "Schizophrenia has fried his brains, do you see? ... *Fried!* His synaesthesia is just one more symptom of his chronic psychotic illness." It was a brutal thing to say. Maybe he was trying to steer me away from disappointment. It was easy to be negative about psychiatry. Theirs was a crude system under a scientific veneer but it was the only thing really in place to stem the outright suffering of mental illness.

After my encounter with the consultant I kept on with Kris in secret, and in some ways I colluded with him in hiding the full extent of his strangeness from the authorities.

He showed his synaesthesia in many forms. Colours had textures as well as sounds. He seemed to live in a multi-stranded world. He liked to watch the jets coming into the local airport. He told me that the sound of their engines made a phosphorescent wake behind them. Words conjured up specific tastes to him. He pointed to McPeake's name on a letter that the hospital had sent him, "That name," he said, "tastes of ear wax," making a wry face. He once indicated a calendar and told me the weeks and months of the year twined around in wreaths of luminescence. Each day had its own corona. He visualised numbers with their own particular colour. They shimmered in dancing sequences to his mind's eye. He seemed to visualise energy waves like vibrating strings beneath the glittering surface of everyday reality. He told me that we all had experienced the mixing of senses when we were infants but most people pruned that gift out of their minds as they got older.

If his world seethed with occult correspondences so he in turn crackled with a strange fierce energy. I had long been on the lookout for someone like Kris among the patients. I had clung to the thought maybe that one of them would be the exception that proves the rule, the extreme of the case by which a general law could be discovered. I thought of Kris's mind as being like one of those primordial volcanic ponds where life on earth first emerged. He certainly looked the part. His intense millenarian gaze swept over you as he waved his large knobby hands about and expounded his ideas. He seemed to fill every corner of his poky housing association flat with passion. Sometimes he'd wrap a bandanna around his head as if to contain all those thoughts rattling around under his great domed brow. He looked to me then like that David painting of Marat. Instead of Charlotte Corday though, for Kris, it should have read 'mental health services'. He rarely took his meds. "Brain poison," he called them. He left unopened strips of chlorpromazine tabs as book markers in many of the texts that he read. He hopped from source to source, taken from libraries and charity shops. Books on the picture writing of American Indians, grammars, tomes on mazes and labyrinths, avionics and thermal physics. He must have consumed several volumes a day. He liked to recite lists, the periodic table, calculus integers, Latin names of British raptors. I asked him how he remembered all those facts.

"I use the Method of Loci," he replied.

"The what?"

"It's a memory house. If I want to remember a thing I put it in a room in my memory house. It's there forever whenever I want to find it."

Sometimes he'd burst out with involuntary squeaks and cries, and locutions in an unknown tongue. I asked him about the strange words he used. He told me it was his own invented language. He called it *Merkitys*. It seemed to go a lot further than the usual portmanteau expressions coined by schizophrenics. Kris's invented system had a structure of its own. He showed me a battered notebook with pencilled columns of vocabulary. It seemed to be made up from Scandinavian roots. He told me that he liked the Finno-Ugric languages because they better expressed the flowingness of things. Glaciers hung on longer in Finland than anywhere else in Europe, he said. I pointed to some pollarded plane trees out on the street and asked him what they were in *Merkitys*. He pursed his lips and said, "Puü." The double vowel held an unexpectedly appropriate, regretful sound.

Perhaps his experiments with language were at one with his synaesthesia. He was fashioning new sensing apparatus to discover the secrets of the universe. He tried to capture it all in long squiggly diagrams he made on rolls of computer paper. I asked him what they were about. "I'm trying to draw a picture of everything," he replied.

"Is that possible, Kris?"

"Oh yes," he said looking up and out his windows at the city cloudscape, "You see, the brain is wider than the sky."

I knew little of his life before he came to be on my case list. He usually deflected personal questions but he told me that he came from the harbour town of Cockermouth in Cumbria. The same place as Fletcher Christian, the Bounty mutineer. He gave no explanation for his Slavonic-sounding last name. Later, I came to view it as a fictional *nom de passage*. It never showed up in computer records whenever I searched for it in later years.

Kris did not present the usual dulling of thought of long-term psychosis. Although he was guarded about his past he was happy to talk about his unusual mental experiences. I once asked him what psychosis was like and he held me in his full-watt stare as he poured out a vivid account. It went something like this, "I know things are going in that direction when I hear the tree roots stirring, feel them writhing, coiling up my feet and ankles. I call it *Nurin* in my language, it means 'inside out'. Mainly it's a scumbling and scuffing of the known world. It comes visiting through whispery scratches and furrows on the surface of things. It is a scraping of a nail on a rough wall. Faint but insistent voices tunnel through those walls. My insides become awash with oracles. They pour out of me. There are petals of fire. Wasps stuttering at orange windows. My blood bubbles like a ten-day-old stew. Dreams run up and down my legs. My veins are mineral, dirt-full like the cracks in an old white cup. Everything seems weird and streaky. My five senses clench and give forth a sixth. I'm as bald as a bird. Razor blades rub at my head. My scalp goes electrical with a glowing charge. What can be salvaged from this wreck? I read and read 'til the pages turn black. Do you get it, do you? No, how can you? You have forgotten what you once knew effortlessly in childhood. Selah!"

It was a privilege to get such a glimpse into his world. I got the impression that people in general were not a priority to him. That, or he had drifted too far to reach out to them. I once asked him about relationships and he replied, "Perhaps love is for the normal. I knew that I was destined to be alone when I once saw my first girlfriend through a frosted glass door. She was all in pieces."

It was not always so easy to communicate with him. He could be paranoid, suspiciously examining his products to see that something special had not leaked out of him. He was forever peering at his mucus after blowing his nose. He used to make a terrible groaning in the lavatory. He would emerge after a long while telling me that he felt his spirit come out of his body whenever his bowels moved. I called round to his place one morning and as soon as I entered the narrow passage leading into his rooms he lunged at me. He pushed me right over and dealt out soft blundering blows to my chest with his great fists. Then, as suddenly, he broke away. I wasn't harmed. Maybe he had become afraid that I was a destroyer come to steal his mind or he was just trying to break through to me. Other times he'd pound his own head in frustration. He'd moan that the antipsychotics had shrunk his brain or the illness was destroying his concentration.

He could get all slowed up and forgetful. Once I became worried that he was starving. His kitchen was full of pans of over-cooked carbonised beans. "Heavy oxidisation," he'd murmured, picking at the congealed lumps. I even took him to a Little Chef on the outskirts of the city as I was concerned about his wasting frame. He ordered a pile of blueberry pancakes but barely touched them. He just gazed outside as if following something in the gesticulation of the wind-swept shrubberies. I asked him what was the matter. *"Kellokült,"* he said in his language.

"What's that mean?" I asked,

"It means clock-debt. You know — lateness. I need to be back studying. There is so little time."

He wanted to spend most of his time making things out of wire and electronic components. That's what he meant by 'studying'. He made wonderful gadgets out of all sorts of bits and pieces. A previous worker told me that Kris had built a computer out of spare parts. I had learned to take his inventions seriously. Early on, he had told me he had made a self-defence machine after being harassed by some local youths. He produced a thing the size of a telephone trailing with wires and with two sharp prongs projecting from one end. I didn't really think that it would work for a moment but advised him that he'd better give it to me as the prongs looked dangerous. Back in the office I was fiddling with it when the sharp ends made accidental contact with my skin and gave me a sizzling jolt. When I told him about it later he just said that I was lucky it was not charged up otherwise the shock I could have received would have been twice that given out by a Taser. After that, I regarded his gadgets with more attention and respect.

It all began to come to a head when he asked me if I knew how he could obtain an aquarium.

"A new hobby, is it, Kris?" I asked.

"Yes, you could say that," he replied.

Chance had it that a colleague was getting rid of some fish tanks and so I obtained them for pennies and brought them to Kris. He just gravely thanked me, lugged them inside and shut the door in my face saying that he had a large project in progress and had no time to talk.

I arrived on my next weekly appointment. Kris was again reluctant to let me in but after some persuasion he allowed me into his sitting room. I was startled to find the entire floor covered with wires and stacks of electronic equipment. The fish tanks were in one corner. Inside the glass I could see brown shapes dashing about in the turbid water.

"What the hell is in there, Kris?" I asked.

"Just fish," he replied airily, "Roach and chub mainly. I netted them in the canal."

"I'm not sure you're allowed to do that,"

"It's a biofeedback system. See the loop," he said, ignoring my concerns.

He pointed to wires emerging from the murky water that led to little dials that looked like ammeters. They flickered with unknown energies. He switched something on at the wall and the room was filled with a low humming sound. The fish jerked about ever more wildly and ranks of lights began to glow in the stacked equipment. In one corner of the room a lattice of cabling led to a row of miniature fans that buzzed frenetically as they cooled another unidentifiable block of electrical components.

"Good heavens, Kris. What is all this for?" I asked.

"Just a prototype. It's all about energy capture." He went to the window stepping over his network of wires and stared up at the sky for a moment. He turned to his equipment and flicked something on. A disembodied voice sounded from a speaker, "This is BA G1781 requesting approach instruction and landing."

"My God, Kris, that's air traffic control!"

137

"Oh yes, I like to speak to them," he said calmly. "You see, the pilots look down on it all. They can see the patterns of the world." He picked up a microphone as if to demonstrate but I persuaded him not to.

"Kris! Don't interfere with aviation. They'll find you and prosecute you. God knows how many laws you've broken with this stuff."

"Oh, I don't think so. They do not trouble dreamers," he replied.

"Why are you doing all this?"

"I'm working towards building a model of the universe. I want to find a general system that sums it all up. What it all means and how it works. You know, the big one. The general model of everything."

"Are you sure you know what you are doing?"

"He who desires and acts does not breed pestilence," he said. That was the nearest he ever came to a joke with me, I think.

He'd promised to show me something special at our next appointment. He told me that he had appreciated the fact that I did not laugh at his efforts. Mainly though, I was worried that he'd endanger the housing block where he lived, or maybe he'd cause some sort of catastrophic power outage on the local grid.

He did not answer the door that next week. Nor the next day. Everything looked dark when I watched his windows in the night. I came back with a housing team and carpenter. We drilled the lock off and entered gingerly. I had found so many clients dead over the years.

The rooms were shrouded in octaves of darkness. There was little mess. Just some old bean cans in the kitchen. Kris had skipped taking everything with him.

I got rung up by the housing association a few days later. The manager told me that Kris had returned his keys by mail. The postmark was a seaside town in Lincolnshire. He'd also sent them a parcel addressed to me. They had seen some wires sticking out of it so they had thought it necessary to call the Bomb Squad. Unfortunately the authorities had performed a controlled explosion. It was all in pieces now. They had said it contained nothing harmful. Did I want it?

I called to collect it as soon as I could. There was a large plastic bin bag with an Explosives Ordnance Disposal sticker on the outside. The contents seemed to consist of a charred shoe box with my name on the lid and a message, just discernible, that read, *The Fire Game of Nil*. The rest comprised a jumble of burnt wires, crumbled circuit switches and fragments of the computer paper upon which he used to draw his diagrams. I could see some words and calculus equations on the blackened paper but it was all mashed up. I spent ages fiddling with those battered remnants but could never get them to fit together coherently. I guessed that Kris had sent me some sort of model of the world as he saw it, a wiring diagram or circuit that explained everything. I worked out what *The Fire Game of Nil* meant though by swapping round the letters but that was as far as I got. I never heard of Kris again. I hope he didn't get snagged up in an asylum someplace. I like to think of him still out there listening to the shape of the rain.

# Nor Shall it Sleep in My Hand

It loomed above us. The blade shone softly in the dim light.

"It's a sabre not a sword," Reg had explained. A sword was for stabbing and this instrument was single-edged, made for slashing. It was for a man on a horse slicing down at a fleeing foe. The weapon dominated the room and we found that our gaze kept returning to it as Reg spoke to us.

He had been one of the city's late summer crop of mad people. Reports had come in that he had been screaming abuse at the local children and banging his head against the walls of his sitting room. The police had been called after he had apparently encouraged his dog to attack his neighbours. Our job had been to assess the risk that he posed to the public. We were from a community protection unit made up mostly of forensic specialists trained in high security hospitals.

He lived at a cluster of bungalows designed for elderly and disabled folk. My colleague, Dr Shafik, and I had surveyed the place before opening the gate. There was no-one to be seen in the adjoining houses. Our footsteps had sounded loudly on the slab path as we approached and rang the door bell. A thick dog chain hung down off a plastic washing line and swung uneasily in the breeze. The chain was attached to a large, studded, empty dog collar. We wondered at what size of canine neck that collar could encompass.

A face appeared at the window then Reg opened the door. He was a heavy man with mounded shoulders under his plaid shirt. His deep-set eyes squirmed behind thick glasses. He faced us for a moment in his narrow hallway like a bear cornered in his den. His head swung from side to side as he glared at us. Then, with a gesture of resignation he led us to his shadowed sitting room. We could hear the dog breathing heavily through its nose in long blasts under an adjoining door. There was also the sound of scratching, heavy claws. Reg indicated to us to be seated. I crouched on the edge of a greasy sofa and Dr Shafik took a recliner chair with grubby floral covers. I hadn't previously worked much with this doctor but we had both been trained in the same system and knew the ropes. We cooperated enough to keep up a connection of shared glances by which we ensured that our visit would be as safe as possible and we were prepared to beat a hasty retreat.

Reg's cave-like room contained little apart from the furniture. There was a sound system in one corner with a

CD cover visible of *Marching Bands of the World.* The walls had several stained dints in them and that was about it — apart from the sole dominating presence of that large, old sabre without a scabbard. It was hooked by two wires quite close to where Reg was standing. The pitted blade gleamed menacingly in the dim light. He could have grabbed it in an instant.

Reg began to tell his story pacing around the room as he spoke. He ignored our attempts to steer the interview and insisted on pressing his version of events on us. He had a forceful voice and he accompanied his account with thrusting gestures from his stubby arms. Whenever we attempted to interject he glared and fumed at us and took a step forward as if about to charge us. We knew much of his personal circumstances anyway from the thick medical notes and so we let him grind on with his painful history.

He had been born in an air force base in Germany but his father had transferred to the experimental unit at Orford Ness on the Suffolk coast where he spent his childhood from the age of nine. The family lived on a forces' estate there. Reg described his lonely school days, shunned by the local boys and marooned with two unhappy parents. His father worked on the bombing ranges doing missile research, or so he told his son, although Reg subsequently learned that he actually was an aircraftsman engaged in retrieving spent rocket casings from the shingle banks and the lagoons around the low-lying spit of land. Reg told us that his father was a silent man who, in his off-duty hours, would take himself away down the shore, just sitting with a bottle, watching the waves go swashing on to the beach.

His mother was another person of few words but she attempted in her own way to compensate for the emptiness of their life together. She took to feeding Reg large, fatty meals. As a boy, he began to hate the taste of lard in everything and the streamers of congealed butter that ran across the plates revolted him. She continued to press her awful dinners on him. He often felt nauseous at the meal table and he began to gag when she tried to make him eat. Reg pressed his broad fingers down his throat and made gargling noises to illustrate to us. He told us he had been taken to see a child psychiatrist in Norwich who diagnosed *emetophobia*, a morbid preoccupation with vomiting. Reg was given tranquillising tablets and his mother advised about meal preparation. The difficulty was only really resolved by Reg eating alone in his room as he did from adolescence onwards. He told us that he would throw much of his food out of his bedroom window to the neighbour's dog and then would exist on snacks bought with his pocket money.

"Animals, they are the only ones that have been good to me," he said, pointing to the kitchen door which creaked under the pressure from the unseen creature beyond.

His chief joy and compensation had been his attendance at the local troop of the Boys Brigade. He loved the sense of order there; the reassuring motto *Sure & Steadfast* on his silver cap badge; the feeling that he was valued by the kindly troop leader and his worth was measured by the proficiency badges that he had won. He told us how his father had been transferred to Scotland but his family did not follow him. Reg's mother came back here to her home town and a replacement figure was installed in time. He was called Uncle Harry. Reg hated him from the outset. Uncle Harry at first attempted to make friends with him. He took him fishing and went with him on a corporation bus to the great October fair in the city. He soon gave up these activities in the face of Reg's sustained hostility and a mutual dislike took hold.

They never spoke and Reg communicated through his mother.

Reg then returned to telling us of his love for the Boys Brigade. How he joined a new group that met at the local Lads' Club. The troop leader there was a middle-aged ex-serviceman whose strong, freckled hands usually grasped a pipe. At first there was comfort in the familiar routines. He earned more bandsman's badges. His special instrument was the snare drum. The troop leader seemed to want to take Reg under his wing. He tutored him on brigade lore in his office — a partitioned box in the drill hall. This cubby hole had filled up with the smell of sweet pipe smoke. There came the first unsettling exploration, a touch on the knee, then rubbing his legs and inner thighs then worse — a hand creeping up the shorts. Sweat would bead the forehead of the troop leader as he groped at Reg and the boy could hear a champing sound as the man's teeth ground at his pipe stem. Reg told us that at first he felt surprise and incomprehension, then he settled to a fearful acceptance. He screwed up his courage to tell his mother about the abuse but something about her blind panicky demeanour when he had previously complained about Uncle Harry prevented him from saying anything in the end.

Reg was not able to tell what was happening to anyone at all, neither to the teachers at school where he became a scowling, disruptive student lagging in his studies, nor to his Brigade comrades who sensed what was happening but said nothing. Still he went to Boys Brigade right through his teenage years. What else did he have? Year on year the troop leader mauled him, picked him out by torchlight in the tent on the brigade camping trips and all the while his anger grew.

Reg paused to puff on an inhaler and he dabbed at his eyes with a large stained handkerchief. I noticed Dr Shafik covertly looking at his watch.

Reg blundered on with his grim biography. How at seventeen he eventually left the Boys Brigade, the troop leader having transferred his attentions to younger boys by then. He wrote to his father whom he believed to be still in Scotland at this time, perhaps hoping to live with him again, but the letter was returned by the Field Post stamped *Transferred — unable to deliver*. Reg then joined the services himself on impulse after visiting a recruiting stand one Saturday afternoon. He was sent to Catterick for infantry training and endured it for three months. Something about the bleak barracks, the 'beasting' by the yelling NCOs and the emptiness of the surrounding bleak moors reminded him of his lonely Suffolk childhood. His control eventually snapped. He went absent without leave and took the train back to the city. On arrival he got drunk in a pub for first time in his life. He came home unexpectedly that night and confronted his mother and raged at her about all the painfulness of his childhood. Uncle Harry pushed him out of the house and they fought together on the lawn outside.

Reg received a beating and retreated. He drank some more beer as his face smarted and he filled up with more anger. At closing time he went to a garage, obtained a two gallon can of petrol and lugged it back through the suburban streets in the winter's night. He poured the petrol onto the front lawn and onto Uncle Harry's car, a little Austin A30. All the while it was quiet except for the gurgle and splatter of the fuel. He recalled the sudden chill on his legs as he soaked his trouser leg, and for some reason he also poured the stuff all over a red pillar post-box which stood by their garden gate. Then he tossed a match onto the grass.

At first there was a yellow trail which went sparking and spluttering back towards him and ran up his trousers where he had dripped fuel onto himself. He had apparently jigged about for a few seconds as the flames flickered up his clothing and seared his hands as he slapped himself in a panicky attempt to put it out. Reg mimed that drama to us. Then he told us how he had lit another match. It had really taken hold that time and an orange flash lit up the street as the car petrol tank suddenly went. Then there was a second louder explosion when the pillar-box blew. Reg had looked up at a piling mass of thick smoke that rose high up and dimmed the street lights. He became suddenly terrified at what he had done. He ran away down the back ways of the housing estate, heading by some instinct to the old Lads' Club drill hall. The building was all locked up but Reg squeezed over a small wooden door to the side of the building and scuttled along to a passage way to the rear where there was a neglected yard. Here he crouched all night until he was found the next day by the caretaker.

This was Reg's offence, his 'index offence', as we in the forensic service called it. He received a sentence of six years in prison, the arson made worse by the mail offence of destroying the letter-box. No-one had been hurt although the exploding petrol tank had taken off all the rendering from the front of his mother's house. He did the first year in a Young Offenders' prison. He worked on a farm there and that was not too bad. However when he reached the age of eighteen he was transferred to adult prison and found himself in a tough, crowded gaol. He was put in segregation for refusing food. A prison officer tried to bully him into eating and Reg lunged at the man, trying to gouge at his eyes with a spoon. After this, he was swiftly transferred to the secure hospital for the criminally insane under a prison transfer order. Thus he had entered our domain.

"It was there at the hospital that really did it, made me bad, still makes me bad so I have a go at the children, and other stuff and it's that place that had made people frightened of me 'cos I do things, stupid things."

Reg stumped over to where the sabre gleamed on the wall and stared up at the weapon as if seeking inspiration. My colleague and I shared glances.

"You know the hospital don't you?" he said turning to us. "I bet they sent you from there. Christ, what bastards you all are!"

Indeed we knew the nearby high security hospital. It was linked to our community service. Dr Shafik had worked there as a staff grade psychiatrist and so had I. Yes, we had been well soused in that sump.

Reg slumped against the wall and put his head into his hands. We could still hear his dog snuffling and scrabbling at the door. Then he raised his bewildered face and told us, "You went up the five steps of the hospital gatehouse lodge. Up the five steps then goodbye to the world boyos."

We knew the official story from the hospital files. We had read about how the hospital had dowsed the fire of his anger through the long years of incarceration to leave him burnt-out and crippled by early arthritis and emphysema. He had been dumped back in the city a few miles from the old family home and site of his index offence. His mother and Uncle Harry were long dead, the troop leader had disappeared to molest children somewhere else and Reg had no other connection to local people. Even the Lads' Club was long boarded-up and due shortly to be the site of a new supermarket.

Reg continued to talk about his past. He evidently needed to get it out even if it was to we indifferent professionals, part of that system that had bound him. "I was there eighteen years in that hospital. They took everything away. The things I could tell you about that place. If the staff didn't like a fellow. Once I was told to clean up on one of the bad wards. I swept up after the staff had had a go at one patient. I found a piece of bloody scalp with the hair attached. I'll never forget sweeping up a piece of that man's head."

Reg gave a gusty sigh.

"Sometimes I think I will go to the press. Tell them what happened."

The sound of children's laughter and loud voices reached us. Youngsters were coming home from school. They were larking about and making whooping noises, being deliberately noisy I would guess, to bait the local ogre. Reg interrupted his reminiscence and went to the window. He peered through the net curtains, muttering to himself and glaring out at his tormentors. His dog, perhaps sensing its master's anger, also began to growl and press against the thin kitchen door. We distracted Reg by asking about his health, getting him to tell us about his bad knees, his breathlessness, his neglect by his doctor who did not understand how disabled he was. He leaned against the wall next to his sabre. For some reason I asked him about the weapon. I ignored Dr Shafik's warning glance to me.

"Ah yes," said Reg, reaching up and picking it off the hangers. He handed it to me. "This was the only thing left to me in my mother's effects. It belonged to an ancestor on my mother's side — a cavalry sabre."

I held it for a moment. It was heavy; its dimpled blade scrolled with antique lettering. The handle was bound with sharkskin held by silver wire. It sat solidly and comfortably in the hand. I wafted the blade for a moment. It felt easy and natural to heft and it was with reluctance that I handed it back to him. There was a little smirk on his face and he had stopped puffing and panting. Our eyes met for a moment then he took it from me and reverently clipped the weapon back on its wire hangers.

In the end we did not intervene with him. Dr Shafik judged him a personality disorder who was probably too fearful of a return to the secure system to offend again. Yes, he was dangerous but it was not policy to treat the untreatable — besides we were supposed to protect his rights to a private life. I did not agree with this approach but Shafik outranked me. We left him to drown in his loneliness, playing his *Marching Bands of the World* CD loudly to spite his meek, frightened, elderly neighbours, raging at his neglectful GP and at the local kids but with the anger slowly being doused by his physical decay.

As Dr Shafik was leaving he had said, "You are really doing well, Reg. You must find positive outlets, take walks in the lovely countryside, find hobbies." His preternaturally white teeth gleamed encouragingly.

Reg glowered at him.

"Yes well, I've seen a lot of you Indian fellows in hospitals also. Good at advice you are," he replied.

Shafik had been content to leave me to handle the aftermath of our visit to see Reg. After compiling our report to his GP and to the police, I took it upon myself to take an unorthodox step and I wrote official letters to the local schools and public agencies warning them to be vigilant about Reg. He must have somehow got wind of this and I was surprised to receive a letter from his solicitor threatening legal action for breach of privacy. Reg was really quite resourceful in his own twisted way. I replied that I had evidence that this man was dangerous and that it was my duty to protect the public and that seemed to have silenced his legal protectors.

Undoubtedly Reg was a victim yet I loathed him and all of his kind. It had seemed somehow harder than ever to stop feeling like this. I had come to a point in my career when I had heard too many of their hard-luck stories. These were outweighed in my mind by all the victim statements, post-mortem reports and crime scene photos that had been thrust upon me. It was as if I in turn wanted to do something to hurt them. Reg's history was indeed a sad one but there were so many like him who had damaged and tormented others. To my mind, they were malign, predatory, and irremediably set wrong — a threat to all tender and vulnerable things.

Reg had somehow done me a favour that day. Allowing me to hold that piece of antique steel was his gift to me. That sabre was like a portent. Its message was that men like Reg were made that way and would never change. My colleagues had quite another view. They believed in rehabilitation, community reparation and the capacity of even the worst to become good citizens. They would have been shocked by my savage rejection of all that. The original institutions where we worked had been built to hold the dangerously mad in perpetuity. It was only the most recent professional generation who saw these men as being curable and forgiveable. My need was to slash through the façade of those new beliefs and to go back down to the bone. And so also, it was I, holding Reg's weapon and cleaving him again and again in fantasy, shearing him from my world and from all that was important to me. Maybe I was the dangerous one then.

Before that summer had ended I put in my resignation from the community protection service.

That was not the last of it. Three or four years later I glimpsed a newspaper billboard which read, *Blade Maniac Strikes!* The TV news showed a large stumpy man being led between minders into court. The camera picked out those blind muzzled features. Yes, it was Reg. He had attacked a repair man who had come to fix the pavement outside his house. The reports said that he had used a sword.

# The Price

There were so many ways to betray the patients. One was to be too out of your head, bombed or whatever, to do a decent job. It didn't matter if you were on booze, puff or pills. If you were intoxicated you were really letting them down. The least you could do for the patients was to pay attention to them in the way they deserved. Even the most limited staff could do that. That's why Sandy had to go. He'd been brought in to do social care reports on high secure patients — people who posed a risk to the public. We used a lot of semi-retired workers like him in those days. They tended to be able to complete the lengthy reports needed for high profile cases whereas the younger staff seemed to come from a post-literate world.

Sandy was a shy man with muddy, bruised features and vague eyes that never settled on you. He spoke with a soft Edinburgh accent. He'd been around the mental health scene for years but I had not worked closely with him. He was inoffensive and meek and quietly got on with his job, but he bothered me. He had absolutely no passion for one thing, not a flicker of enthusiasm for the job. I was used to burnt-out workers, but normally they showed at least the echo of the feelings they once held. Sandy gave out nothing. I knew something was not right so I kept an eye on him and took to popping into his office unexpectedly. The other staff had got used to me keeping tabs on them. I was the tough new boss brought in from acute services to sort out this backwater office. I wasn't popular. I scrutinised their practice, stopped them from smoking in their offices and questioned their travel claims. The head of service had been too gentle to keep discipline, and mischief had thrived in the vacuum.

Sandy kept me at bay for a while. His reports were adequate so I couldn't pick him up on those. He was always shuffling about the department with a pipe and cradling an ever-present thermos of coffee. His room smelt of stale shag even weeks after I'd banned him from smoking in there. One day I watched his narrow back going up through the security turnstiles to the locked wards, then I had a chance for a good look around in his room. I sat in his chair and scanned his desk. There was a litter of chunky blue case files, a computer with a dusty screen and some index cards with lists of phone numbers. I tried the drawers and found them locked. Poked around and found his key hidden in a stapler box. I worked my way down through the desk. Just looking. I wasn't sure for what. I unearthed an old tin containing humbug mints and a wooden heraldic shield with a clan emblem. When I couldn't see anything else in his scanty personal effects, I pulled out his thermos, kept snug in a deep lower drawer. Something made me unscrew it and take a sniff. It might have looked like coffee but from the smell it was mostly vodka. That was it. Old Sandy was evidently pickled most of the time. It all became clearer. His careful, tortoise-like, crabbing gait had evidently evolved to stop him from falling over dead drunk. You couldn't smell the alcohol on him because of that vile pipe tobacco. I informed the head of service. I had some other inadequate staff in my sights as well. I wanted the best and they didn't fit. You needed a good team in view of the risks of the clientele. The head of service shrank from taking action but I prodded him into it. Sandy was on a temporary contract so no bother. I watched him hobbling away to the car park with his desk things in a box a few days later. I even gave him a Judas handshake in farewell. At the time I didn't think twice about it. I accepted occasional weaknesses in workers but I didn't want long-term liabilities. I justified it to myself but in reality my own betrayals had been so much worse than Sandy's. Maybe I was punishing him for stuff I had done myself.

***

It was ten years or so before. It doesn't really matter how I got into it. I had been ready to go to the wild side. I had romantic notions and thought that I was an explorer. There was a hole at my centre and something had to fill it up. It had started as a weekend habit but pretty soon it had become an everyday thing. I couldn't wait to go home to get wired. I was working in a community mental health team and thought I was coping but really a constant hunger kept building through the day to a frantic pitch. As soon as I'd gone through my front door I'd shed my work stuff and light the gas ring. I'd take out a transparent sachet of grey-brown powder kept hidden in an edition of *Fleurs du Mal*. The bag of works was usually stashed at the back of the fridge. I'd pull off a ball of cotton for a filter. A slice of lemon sluiced through the syringe usually sufficed to clean the barrel. I would shoot thirty units of water to mix with the powder. Cooked it in the tarnished bowl of an old spoon on the gas flame. Not too much or you'd boil it all off and lose the shot. Drew it up through the cotton. Had a quick look at the amber liquid swirling around in the barrel. Tried not to focus on any black bits spinning there. They were impurities from the cut. Offered a prayer that they'd not lodge somewhere and give me an embolism. The ligature would set the arm throbbing. I had good veins anyway. Hit the spot, watched the telltale plume of blood. Loosed the binding, pushed the plunger in and out in to balance it then — *Boff!* Pushed it all the way in. Falling, falling, dropping backwards into a feather bed a mile deep.

The junkies I knew called me "a chipper". I was chipping in and out, not a serious user. It felt serious though. Those strange empty mornings after being on the stuff. Waking with a sense of déjà vu, a grey mineral dust settling on everything. All the sounds oddly muffled. Shapes flickering at the corner of my vision, but whenever I turned my head — nothing there. Driving to work, the songs on the radio seemed to boom distantly like waves on a lonely shore. The only clear thing was my internal voice. I kept repeating phrases to myself, obscure fragments of verse mainly. One I remember was a line from Verlaine. *It wounds my heart with a monotonous languor.* I kept repeating it like a prayer. *A monotonous languor.* The words mirrored those fuzzy days.

On heroin you felt right for the first time in your life. All pain and care dropped away. You were lying back as on a boat, propped up on soft cushions, gliding through the black channels of lucid dreams.

I shifted away from using the needle after a while. It was too risky even for me. I took to smoking the stuff off cooking foil instead. A technique called chasing, chasing the dragon to use the full melodramatic phrase. The rush was not as deep and chasmal as mainlining but the dreams were just as good and you could prolong the hits. I'd sit smoking all the summer night on my back porch, with the moon a yellow gob and the clouds rolling out like cannon smoke.

First of all it was about how good you feel on it, then it was how bad you were when you were off it. Once those morphine metabolites had latched into your body chemistry then you had a habit that would not go away easily. Quite soon, if you hadn't smoked for a day, you'd get a crawly-ants feeling over your skin, a chill in your gut and a dripping nose. You'd feel old and itchy and would start coughing and rubbing your legs because the bones ached. That was called "clucking" by the junkies. I called it "whining". Those dreary moaning junkies. How I hated them. Always complaining. They were like sponges in the desert. All dried up by their habit. No feelings really, just intensely selfish beings. Checking in the mirror all the time to see how pinned their eyes were, speaking in grating voices, always wanting to talk about how to get over-the-counter stuff to bolster their habit. Their talk droned on about DF118s, Vicodin, cough syrup or Collis Brown. Pharma shit. I was disgusted at the company I kept. But still I'd score off them and went on with it.

I thought I was still working conscientiously but the patients drifted past me like ghosts. I was short-changing them by my inattention. I used to do home visits to see a schizophrenic woman. She was a gentle soul who was a keen photographer but with an odd choice of subject matter. Her mantelpiece was covered with photos she had taken of her mother on her death bed. I used to sit for hours with her as she chattered away and I drifted in hazy reverie. She once insisted on taking my photo. She printed it off and gave it in at the office. I still have it. There I sit with a papery face and wonky eyes, framed behind by the pictures of her dead mother. It gave me a bit of a jolt, getting that photo. I looked awful. Nearly as bad as her mum.

Not content with evenings and weekends, my habit crept into the day. Mid-morning I'd get fidgety and leave the office. Drove the car to the tree line by some out-the-way playing fields. Burned the tarry trails of junk on sheets of foil and sucked up the metallic smoke. Lolled back and watched the spider webs spooling off the sheltering limes. Swirly dots fogged my vision. They were tiny worm eggs which then turned to furry bees tunnelling out of my eyes. The insects spun around my head then covered the windscreen. Everything went dark. I leaned forward and rubbed the glass. The bees had turned to dust. Sad, cosmic dust. My fingers squeaked loudly as I rubbed. I was trying to make a hole for the sun to shine through.

I'd get back to the office after an hour, or was it a day? I furtively searched my colleagues' faces to see if they had noticed anything. Afternoons I'd keep checking my face in the toilet mirrors.

The beginning of the end came when I crashed my car one night. I was wired, listening to music and just following the road without thought. All of a sudden stop lights slid past. I felt unable to react and went right across a busy junction between fast traffic and over an embankment the other side. The car took off for a moment. I had a clear image of a ploughed field lit by my descending headlights. The gods of skag protected me. The car landed upright with a groaning crash, the tape deck still playing as a haze of dust obscured the wreckage. The police tested me for drink afterwards but never noticed my pinned eyes.

A week later I bought a large amount of methadone from a dealer for three hundred quid. His entire stock. Those square-ended white tabs with an M incised on them were going to be my own detox method. I couldn't ask for help from the professionals you see, because I was one of them.

Methadone was crippling stuff. You felt like the living dead on it. It was fairly poisonous and after I'd taken my morning dose I often had to stop my car on the way to work and spew into some poor citizen's front garden. Days on that crap felt like a damp frigid hand always clamping at your belly. It took away the intensity of junk longings though and so I plugged on with it, gradually lowering the dose each day through that long winter. I started on sixty mg a day and by February I was grinding the tablets into quarters as I titrated the dose down as far as I could bear. I kept the last tabs in an old coffee jar and by the end I was licking the dust at the bottom just to get a faint buzz to quell the heaving chill in my innards. Four months into detox and it was all gone. The habit had departed, a conquered king passing furiously away, leaving yawning sightless days in his destructive wake.

It took years to get over it. Whatever junk gave me left a vacuum within. I shored myself up with an unbending work persona, encased in a grim dedication to my job. A hardness developed. I never took a day off sick again. Those drug testing dogs used to sniff at my legs during snap checks in the maximum security institutions where I worked. That amused me and I smiled darkly at the stolid dog handlers. I laughed during drugs conferences at the naivety of the earnest ignorant lecturers. I occasionally encountered junkies at work. That was comic. They whined, "You don't know what it's like, man." That poison had made me intolerant. Something dies in you when you turn your back on so much visceral pleasure. Maybe that was the real price of the stuff. It also killed the youth in me. I had drank from Lethe and forgot all else. I was never coming home again. I chose to work in jails or high secure places. I loved 'em. It felt familiar there. Dead hours. Corridors of lostness.

\*\*\*

So, sorry about that, Sandy. You too will have to heal yourself I guess — or go under. It was nothing personal. I had the intolerance of the survivor. The cruelty of self-help bred small forgiveness. Time anyway just noses at the carcase of the present for a while then it moves on.

# The Happiest Country Has No History

They found him in an out-of-season, Norfolk holiday resort, a hundred miles from home.

He'd travelled to the sea's edge and found moorage on a bench by the lifeboat station. He'd been there several days at least. They were not really sure how long. The boarded-up arcades had given him shelter and hidden him from the security cameras. He seems to have survived on chips bought at the King Cod restaurant that was still open. He'd probably kept a little money on him but had not used his cash card. Otherwise they'd have tracked him sooner.

I imagined him hunkering there under a serene neutral sky, registering dawn's lume and the slow encroach and retreat of the tide. At night, just the clinking of wind-stirred bulb strings in the defunct amusements park and the creaming sibilant breakers far out beyond the estuary. He'd found a good place with no constraint, there by the shining amnesic Norfolk mud.

He had gone missing a week before. His photo had been publicized in newspapers and on the TV. His features showed the same sort of hopeful unwitting look you see in pictures of soldiers killed in small pointless wars. We don't know how he got as far as Norfolk. His car was found on a dead-end fenland track near to his home. It was quite close to a wind turbine farm. The searchers tried to trace his passage between the cabbage fields and those stark, gyring contraptions. It didn't look good at that stage so they'd used poles to probe the dykes and drains for him. All the while he'd been making his way to the sea. They had no idea how he got there. Maybe sleep walkers were invisible. There was a loosening of gravity somehow and he had just popped up by the coast.

We saw him in psychiatric outpatients. He had been brought back by an ambulance with escorts. Quite a young man, vaguely surprised at all the attention. We asked him his name. Name? He shrugged, reluctant to get into the detail. He stared back at us, polite but somehow disinterested. We tried another tack and offered him his name.

"Yes, that's me," he replied. He yawned then rubbed the back of one hand with the palm of the other. Then he looked down at his lap as if his name was sitting there like a stone. He was called Tull, fittingly for a history teacher. He hadn't recognised it when they first found him but now he accepted his name. It was him, yes "Tull", or a version of him. Maybe he saw everything differently

160

after his quiet epiphany by the sea in Norfolk and names were no longer very important. He looked up again at us with pale, stunned eyes. He had untidy thick hair and ruddy wind-roughened cheeks. He was dressed in a check shirt and Barbour jacket. There was an old-fashioned rural look to him. He could have been a ghillie or a gamekeeper, I thought.

There was no immediate evidence of drink or drugs. We took a liver function test and a full blood count to check further. There was no head injury, no psychosis, nor mood disorder. His neurology seemed grossly normal and there wasn't any obvious epilepsy. We probed gently about the circumstances of the day that he disappeared. Classes had been winding down before February half term. He had been about to take some boys for rugby on a Wednesday afternoon. It was a state school with grammar school pretensions in the green suburbs. He'd been driving to the sports field and that was the last he could remember. We rooted for trauma. No, he had no particular worries, no scandals, no evident rattling skeletons. His wife was also a teacher. They lived in a bungalow and kept a Labrador dog. There was nothing apparently sinister that had happened at school. Tull had a good reputation as a teacher. The couple had no evident problems although the wife had acknowledged that they had mildly quarrelled about having a baby. The only thing of note was that it was the anniversary of his father's death from renal disease two years before.

We'd seen him as a pair of clinicians. It was an unusual case and because of the publicity the hospital was cautious. We suspected a fugue state and took turns asking our questions. Usually someone experiencing a dissociative fugue will have been jolted into that condition by some troubling event or person who may have connected them to early life trauma. In that sense the fugue was like a shield or armour against the psychic distress. The fugue state, implied movement, an acting out of a dissassociative trance. You usually saw sudden, unexpected travel away from home, coupled with an inability to recall one's past and a confusion about personal identity. Sometimes a new identity was assumed altogether. The dissociative flight could be accompanied by significant distress. Tull did not seem troubled nor could he identify any precipitating event. It was clear though that he had made some sort of inward journey to a place where language had failed.

We continued to pick away at him in order to nail down a diagnosis although it wasn't easy. Fugue was a psychogenic state that superimposed onto the hard wiring of the brain. It could only be proved by showing what it is not. It was a diagnosis that was confirmed only when the sufferer had returned to their ordinary life. That was another problem — the text books spoke of the fugue patients returning to their 'ordinary lives' but I somehow doubted that things would ever be the same for Tull again. He seemed to have been changed by his dream journey. Perhaps it had been a sort of vision quest. He had touched other sources of being.

He didn't quite match the diagnostics but it was unusual to see a fugue state. I had only encountered it a couple of times in my whole career. My fellow clinician and I left the interview room to have a discussion about what to do with him. If it was fugue then there was no real treatment. Psychotherapy can sometimes help by working on a person's insight about how they cope with life's challenges. Especially when the fugue journey seems to be an expression of an unconscious wish to escape from a pressured life. Tull however didn't give us much to work on. He seemed so vague as if his fugue state had removed the conventional desires and disappointments that usually perplexed the rest of us. We thought it wise to put him on a ward and do more tests. We could see him still sitting in the interview room. His seemed smitten by his own inner tides. His wife brought him a hot drink and switched on the room light. He stared up at the flicker of the neon tube in sickly surprise as if looking at such a thing for the first time. I tried to imagine his fugue journey. We've all been taken in our dreams to a good place, a utopia where everything is happy and whole. Perhaps Tull's body had obeyed a dream calling. In that way the flesh can be more elastic than the mind.

I'd read somewhere that 'utopia' came from the Greek for no place, *où topos.* So, all those that have seen utopia as an 'ideal society' may have it wrong. Utopia was within the self, not other people. It was really a *no place,* somewhere excluded to those like me whose minds were clouded by all that scrutinising self-knowledge and too much attention to things. *No place* was just a zone where there were no events, only processes. Water falling, grasses moving, clouds unrolling. A demesne of furious dreaming.

Well, we told Tull he'd probably experienced fugue and it likely wouldn't happen again. We offered precautionary admission which he refused and we did not have enough to section him. He reluctantly agreed to a follow-up appointment. There was a strange firmness to him underneath that vague exterior. He was like a traveller given new confidence by a pilgrimage to the centre of his being.

For some reason I followed them out of psychiatric outpatients along the bustling corridors of the big general hospital. They threaded through the crowded concourse, Tull and his wife, walking along steadily. Past the hospital shop where tired nurses and bumptious young doctors, wearing their stethoscopes on their shoulders, queued for confectionery, energy drinks and celebrity gossip mags with bright covers. Flashes of early spring sunlight came off windscreens from the car parks beyond. That's where I lost sight of them and felt a strange pang of loss. I had envy for where Tull had been. Maybe we all need to go to fugue land.

Whenever I think of him I return to a childhood holiday. The Falls of Shin in the far Scottish north lands, the Kyle of Sutherland. Watching the summer salmon blindly leaping up the peaty darksome runnels, silvered, straight from the sea, nosing the impossible.

# The Drowned and the Saved

Who are they to me, the dead? Their faces bob in my memory like drowned souls after a flood. It is at night particularly that I think of them. Alone in my study, putting off the small slice of extinction that is sleep. Outside the moon drifts, radiant with terror. Night moths fidget at the window. I'm not sure myself what the dead mean to me but they certainly remain, refusing to leave. Sometimes they seem to be at the back of me, just huddled. There is no communication, nothing spooky like that although in my youth I tried that ouija stuff, the spinning cup and tilting table. No, they are just there, hanging around in the background. I can't get rid of them even if I wanted to. I'm not looking for disposal or a settlement though. I just want to find a way of living on with them. I want space for all of us. Why should I feel this way about them? Perhaps it is something to do with responsibility. These dead that stay with me came under my charge at one time. They were my clients, patients, customers, the descriptor changed with the times. They were on my case list. That was something of my choosing rather than theirs. I had agreed to take them on in one way or another and they were the ones I could not save. It's not that I feel guilty about them. None of them really had a chance from the beginning. Nor did they die by my sins of omission or commission directly although I was undoubtedly involved in some way in their demise. I just feel liable for them. I was answerable for their care. I do not think like this about those of my colleagues who also died, so many of them whittled away by illness, stress and suicide. They do not haunt me. They always had choices and that made all the difference. No, it's my old case load that has followed me, quietly taking their places and refusing to leave. Most often I ignore them, other times they are just part of the lumber room of the past. Some nights though I want to see them more distinctly. It is hard to make them out. Their faces wobble and blur. Like looking into an old fumed aquarium tank, I rub at the glass to make out the misty, reluctant inhabitants inside.

\*\*\*

Iris was one of my first clients. A great lump of a Down's Syndrome girl with long silky hair falling each side of her round skull from a cleft-like parting. She never spoke except for a lisping, barely discernible, "Yes," which she answered to most questions. If she did not like whatever was being proposed then her face just assumed a bewildered grimace. She spent her days in the therapy centre

166

quietly doing simple tapestry or needlework, the blunt wedge of her tongue protruding in concentration. This was one of those old-fashioned places where those with a learning disability were herded together to pass their time in harmless activity while the busy world ran on without them. She liked to sit by me as I filled out the registers and care plans and whenever I looked up she would give me a timid smile. I began to quite enjoy her presence and thought of her as my mascot, a sort of smiling Buddha. It was my first care job. The day centre was run mainly by ex-servicemen with fixed notions about how the work should be done. Much emphasis was put on fire safety and there were monthly fire drills.

Iris was considered too fat, slow or confused to be able to respond in time to an emergency and I was told that it was my job to drag her on a large piece of cardboard all the way to the fire exit. The piece of board was kept stowed behind a radiator and Iris and I practised once a month. When the bell sounded I would regretfully draw it out and Iris lowered herself down and lay there on her back like an up-ended beetle. I was too young or stupid to question this practice so we persevered for the months that I knew her. Puffing and blowing, I'd drag her all the way down one long corridor across a dining room then outside onto a concrete path. We were always the last to arrive. Everyone else would be kept waiting for our ignoble scraping arrival.

After each practice great tears would roll down her cheeks. Whether this was due to the indignity or the discomfort or both I did not know. I would try to think of things to cheer her up. What I said had to require the answer, "Yes." For example, "Sunny day isn't it, Iris?" Or, "Lovely flowers, Iris?" I knew when she was in better spirits because she'd come and present me with a choco-late teacake, spangled with hundreds and thousands, usually with a deep thumb print embedded in its shiny top. She used to make the cakes in domestic science classes. I always let her eat as many of the surplus cakes as she liked. I didn't see the point in restricting her although there were uneasy thoughts when I waved her off on her bus home and heard later that she had keeled over with a heart attack while descending the steps. Those disabled day centre clients died like wasps in autumn but Iris was the first client and my favourite.

***

Chris, a male cross-dresser, raw-boned and gawky. Before I ever worked with him I used to see him tottering into the city in the evenings on high heels with his great knotted legs pumping along under a miniskirt, his platinum blond wig, worn slightly askew, shimmering under the street lights. The lads on nights out would jeer at him but he seemed to take no notice just staring ahead and constantly talking to himself. He joined my case load after concern had built up that he was neglecting himself. Apparently he had once married a woman who was very much older than himself. When she had died he had coped with the grief by wearing her clothes and then progressed to more striking female attire. Despite his startling appearance Chris was as shy as a woodland creature and very hard to track down. He would never answer the door in his tower block flat and I could only get in by hovering in the dank corridors until he returned from one of his mysterious journeys and catching him on his door step. I only managed to enter his place a few times. He lived in stunning squalor. The whole flat was packed with debris to chest height. Chris wended his way through narrow paths in the compacted mess. He never seemed unhappy as such, just oddly disconnected, trilling pop tunes to himself in falsetto, making inconsequential remarks and asking me curious questions like,

"God is watching us from far away, he is moving from us because we have disappointed him. Don't you think?" There was a strange charm and beauty to him with his beaky nose poking out under the blond fringe of his wig. Even though I disconcerted him by my persistent visits he was always charmingly polite to me, excusing himself as he edged away from me, "Must be away, I have world affairs to discuss." Things got worse though. He became thinner and more erratic. He would stand for hours at the cosmetics counters of local department stores quizzing the sales girls for beauty tips until they became uneasy and called the police. He became even more elusive.

Eventually I persuaded my colleagues that we should section him on the grounds of acute self neglect. We broke his door down one morning to find him singing to himself on a filthy sofa shadowed by the towering heaps of rubbish. He did not seem surprised or angry but he made us wait until he had put on his make-up before he allowed us to take him to the ward. I hoped at least that we could use the interlude to clean his flat and build him up a little. I got a call a few hours later. Shortly after arriving on the ward he'd had a severe asthma attack and had died in that large hospital with no-one able to stop it. I guess his germs had proved to be so much less lethal than hospital cleanliness. I felt it was my fault.

The relatives who had disowned him in life chased me for years because there was a rumour that he had thousands of pounds hidden somewhere in all that rubbish. If it ever was there then it went with everything else to the council tip.

*** 

Alan always resisted seeing himself as my client. He just wanted to talk in a friendly way. He was desperately lonely but never liked to admit it. I was going through one of many crises at the time and I wonder if I saw in Alan something of a future self so I tended to him with superstitious care. He drank too much and was prone to melancholia. A garrulous middle-aged Geordie, he had survived two marriages and a career in the air force but life on his own in a council estate was a torture.

I saw him for about four years in his poky book-lined place, all felted in grey dust. I used to spend regular Wednesday afternoons there, his seamed red apple face in a haze of roll-up smoke, telling me long convoluted stories of the past or describing books he liked. His favourites were his collection of "fifty tales". These were a long-forgotten series of publications from the 1930s. Thick books with grainy black covers. *Fifty Amazing Stories of Heroic Deeds, Fifty Enthralling Tales of the Mysterious East* — that sort of thing.

He was a man who was thrilled by the amazing but he never could transcend his surroundings. He had a talent for friendship though, and I think he liked to entertain me. He thought up little japes like donning a Father Christmas outfit once after we had both groused about the horrors of the season. In the end I couldn't justify the time I was giving him and allocated the case to a new worker, a young woman, attractive, bright and plausible, bustling with good ideas.

Alan gave me a look of gentle reproach when I told him.

"You're giving me a lass, a wean that knows naat," he had said. Well, that wean soon saw him out. In supervision she used to briskly report all the things she was doing for Alan, benefit advice, health checks, leisure ideas. I even felt a twinge of self-criticism, maybe I should have done a better job with him. This was dispelled when the police rang. Alan had been found dead in his flat. He had

170

probably been lying there for weeks. The neighbours had eventually called them when they'd seen the black mass of flies at the windows. I sifted through the young worker's case notes. Her accounts of her home visits ran in a neat detailed hand. I was sure that they were fabrications and that she actually had rarely bothered to see him. He was probably lying dead already on the days that she had noted: *DV completed. Client A in good spirits. Nil concerns of note. Advice given on obtaining library card and attending Well Man clinic.* I suspended her but couldn't prove malpractice. She found a job elsewhere because I would never let her return to where I worked.

***

Kevin is the one I see the most clearly, yet he is the most mysterious. I see his hands particularly, his capable hands, long-fingered and handsome, flecked with fine blond hairs. Those hands that time and again took up the instruments that would hurt him. His gaze also, which changed with his moods from blue as chipped ice when he was intent and hostile or to a soft sea-green in his boyish, good-humoured everyday self.

I took him on because something had to be done. As an adolescent he had started to climb tall buildings and threaten to jump. Police and the fire brigade had to be called and Kevin was coaxed or dragged down. These episodes were expensive in man hours and were causing disturbances. Large crowds would gather. Some used to urge him to jump and be done with it. He then upped the ante and was found running along a narrow parapet of a road bridge eighty feet above the great brown river that ran through the city. A policewoman had prevented his seemingly inevitable plunge by handcuffing herself to him. The newspapers had called her *The Angel of the Parapet.*

Psych assessors pored over him. Kevin stared blandly back. They were puzzled by him. He denied low mood, feelings of angst or distress and there was no evidence of delusions or odd thought processes. He just did those dangerous things because he felt like it at the time. There was no real trauma or abuse, no psychic horrors in his past. His working-class family were as mildly dysfunctional as any other. They pinned a label of Axis Two, Cluster B personality disorder on him. A borderline or emotionally unstable PD. Then they retreated. There was no real treatment offered. That's when I started with him. My approach was to hang onto him, to encourage stability in his flowing world and to get him to live in and appreciate the present moment. I sought never to remind him of the problematic past but always to move him on, to pray for maturity and a settling of his quicksilver sense of self.

I think that Kevin had no real idea of his personal domain. No shape, no sense of the space he occupied. He was a handsome lad with thick fair hair always styled in a differing ways. His hands were restless, usually fiddling or twisting at something. He never worked, never really belonged to the active world. Most days he'd lie in front of the luminous eye of the telly.

In later years he acquired a girlfriend who then became a wife. They had a child but still the explosions kept coming. Those slim hands kept ripping into packs of tablets, feeding himself dangerous overdoses of painkillers, or hanging from high window sills or even, once, an electricity pylon.

He took up an axe and started fighting with the local thugs. He showed me a slash across palm of his hand given him by a Bowie knife from one of his street adversaries. He had a look of quiet satisfaction then. Maybe he only felt truly alive and in control during those explosive moments. The rest of the time he had an *accidie* that ate up all joy. His doting woman tidied and cleaned after him as he lay about and she bore his child, but his gaze would chill to crystal whenever he spoke of her. Love just washed off him. I always knew he'd die young though I struggled to prevent it. So many times sitting by his hospital bed seeing his fair hair on the pillow next to a tangle of tubes accompanied by the hiss of oxygen.

"Don't die, Kevin. Don't die," I'd whisper. I just wanted him to see the world as wonderful and find something good to hold onto. There were signs of hope. He began to show an interest in gardening. He agreed to start a horticulture course and took pride in showing me the lines of wallflowers he had sown in his little garden. He started to walk in the lush grounds of the great university that was nearby. He got a thrill from evading the security guards but told me he felt peaceful there especially in a new garden they were building to celebrate the millennium. That's when we parted. I had to go to a new job. He assured me that all would go well for him as I fussed over him that last time like an anxious parent. He waved farewell to me from his sunlit garden, his washing jittering in the wind on the line behind him.

I had warned those that followed me in notes and letters that Kevin needed to be watched and to be held but his diffidence and his blank boyish charm lulled them into an unwise complacency and he was soon discharged from active follow-up. He was only offered a monthly ten minute slot in clinic from a disinterested foreign junior doc. He apparently soon stopped attending. Life began to throw up a series of insults and problems. An alignment of factors occurred — relationship difficulties mainly — but it didn't really take much to upset Kevin.

A medic I had once worked with rang me to tell me about it. She had seen my name in the notes during the subsequent enquiry and she thought I should know what had happened. It had been New Year's Eve, a fresh century dawning. Kevin apparently took himself up to the university millennium gardens just before midnight. Those hands fashioned a noose with the washing line from his garden. He looped the line over a modish sculptured archway shaped like a kite wing. It overlooked a circular dark pool and further off the outlines of black trees and the great bowl of the city. And that was that as they say. I still go up there sometimes looking out at the same view from the archway. I think now that he only felt truly omnipotent and in control of his life in those last moments of existence. I imagine that he kicked himself off just as the barrage of fireworks went up on the stroke of the new century.

\*\*\*

So there they are in their form and particularity as I remember them. May they have peace. We live now in hasty times where the old ceremonies are withered away. No requiem or kaddish for these. I had arrived five minutes late to Iris' funeral in a country church yard. They were already finishing as I hurried up, a few mourners filing away and a little yellow digger beginning to fill the hole. Chris also had a brief chapel service. There was no allusion to his real self in the funerary address. His stolid family that had disowned him in life sat all down one side and glared at me, the sole mourner. Alan was burned anonymously in the local crem with little fuss. Kevin was buried long before I found out that he had actually died. Still with no headstone after so many years, Kevin has now just a tilting wooden cross and the remains of some weather-eroded silk flowers.

All we have is the shaping mirror, the house of words. My poor dead clients exist in my curved lens alone. I have bound them there. I am the only help left to them. Not the plangent ceremonies of old beliefs nor the ouija board releasing the jerky frenzy of the dead. Just the mirror of my memory. A bridge for the dead to pass along. May someone in time also do that for me. My eyes get tired from so much grieving and turmoil. I see Iris with her Buddha smile, Chris in his high heels on St James Street, Alan in his Christmas hat with a sly amused look, Kevin playing with his son in his garden. Because I think of them and not myself I can smile now and ready myself for sleep.